"The hope of Polish literature."

—*Frankfurter Allgemeine Sonntagszeitung*

★ ★ ★

"Promise me something, Fah," she said one day as they were on their way to get coffee at that utterly trendy Bad Berry, where various oddballs sit out the livelong day, exposing the world to their exceptionality, the crux of which, it turns out later, is situated in their glasses frames . . . The coffee's coffee, no revelation tastewise, and Fah thought that she might be out of her mind to be paying eight dollars for a regular coffee. Out the window stretched a view onto dusty Bath, opalescent in the heat, full of commotion and afternoon bustle, of mothers with children and schlubby hipsters in alpine caps despite the heat, with bags that recalled old scrota. "Promise me something, Fah," Joanne said. "From now on we're done with ratty old boys, okay? No more boys, no more socks, no more sound of them scratching their balls in the sleepless night. Promise me. Death to douchebags!"

★ ★ ★

"A wild, technicolor send up of culture and consumerism."

—Caitlin Luce Baker, Island Books

ALSO AVAILABLE BY DOROTA MASŁOWSKA

Snow White and Russian Red
translated by Benjamin Paloff
(Black Cat/Grove Atlantic)

Honey, I Killed the Cats

Dorota Masłowska

TRANSLATED FROM THE POLISH
BY BENJAMIN PALOFF

Deep Vellum Publishing
Dallas, Texas

Deep Vellum
3000 Commerce St., Dallas, Texas 75226
deepvellum.org · @deepvellum

Deep Vellum is a 501c3 nonprofit literary arts organization
founded in 2013 with the mission to bring
the world into conversation through literature.

Originally published as *Kochanie, zabiłam nasze koty*
by Noir sur Blanc, Warsaw, Poland, in 2012

First edition, September 2019

Work on this translation was generously supported by a fellowship
from the National Endowment for the Arts.

Published simultaneously in Canada
Printed in the United States of America
ISBN: 978-1-941920-82-4
eISBN: 978-1-941920-84-8

LIBRARY OF CONGRESS CONTROL NUMBER: 2019948093

Cover Design by Anna Zylicz | annazylicz.com

Typesetting by Kirby Gann

Text set in Bembo, a typeface modeled on typefaces cut by Francesco Griffo
for Aldo Manuzio's printing of *De Aetna* in 1495 in Venice

"*Cats!* It's about cats . . . You'll love it." —Roy Cohn

CHAPTER I

There was a white-ruffed cat lying in the street in front of the apartment building, neither warming itself in the sun, nor really even alive, as we might surmise from the fact that there was no sun, nor any other reason to lie there among speeding cars. *Some patrol will eventually come and take him away,* Farah thought in her dream, and, tugging at her pajama bottoms, which had given her a wedgie, she went back to reading her magazine.

She had just been taking a personality test, and . . . Well, it's not like in your life it's always the time and place to be reading Sartre in the original from upside down to around the back, is it? She had been wandering around a set slapped together from bits of university campus and pieces of former apartments, familiar staircases, streets, and other scraps of the past, when this copy of *Yogalife* fell into her hands.

Oh, a new issue, she thought, surprised, since the last one had come out just a couple days before. Flipping through it—"Yogastyle," "Meditation: We Select the Best Gadgets!"—she had happened upon this test.

"Yoga and You: Friends or Bitter Rivals?," "Are You a Sexy Yogi?," and so on—you get the idea. But barely had she marked her first response when she noticed a small, rose-colored slip of paper written with strained carelessness, with stylized urgency . . .

"See you in class on Wednesday . . ." the note announced. The font changed a bit further on, and everything was written in a heated whisper, as if it were in French. F. didn't know French, but that's precisely what she sensed in her ear and much, much deeper than that: ". . . maybe we could meet for coffee, you know the place . . . I want to watch as you drink cappuccino and that silly foam mingles with the lipstick on the rim of your mug, oh yeah . . ." ". . . every day I think of throwing a bouquet of flowers into your car and booking it, just booking it like a puppy, so that all you'd see is my back disappearing into the crowd, my backpack bouncing in an awkward sort of way, a vulnerable sort of way . . ."

"But . . . but I . . ." Farah says, turning the love jottings in her hands. It has left her breathless. So all those days that she'd thought were empty, unremarkable, and pointless, days that had cast her like a diseased fish onto the shore of a solitary evening . . .

For the moment, the fact that she didn't have a car somehow slipped her mind.

. . . all those hellish days whose soundtrack consisted of the whining of teakettles and the dings of her neighbors' microwaves announcing their frozen hamburgers' arrival at "repulsive, and warm to boot!"; lunchtime conversation from behind walls, recalling in its dispassionate timbre a language course in which the same lesson ("What's new at school?" "For the love of God, pass me the cheese knife.") is replayed ad infinitum, out of thriftiness, or else maybe that's all the words and things there are to say in the language of those sleepy, defeated late September afternoons . . .

Days that she'd taken for lost, days when she'd felt like air that was slightly thicker and English-speaking, it must have been then that someone had been watching her the whole time, following her, dazzled by her existence, going crazy over her and . . .

"I can still see the line of the seam in your pantyhose . . . I think about when I'll get to see for myself whether it's a seam or just drawn with a Sharpie on your lotioned calf, shiny as glass, and whether I might someday slide my tongue along it, all the way to . . ."

But I don't wear pantyhose with seams, she suddenly realized, releasing the sheet of paper, which immediately fluttered and fell among the autumn leaves, half-eaten chicken wings, dog shit, and crumpled Starbucks cups. Where it was immediately picked up by Frank, that dude from her yoga class, the one she really quite liked. He was wearing a natty gray sweater and a tidy little collar, his magnificent teeth were shining in the September sun like the keyboard of some expensive instrument, and you could smell the aroma of his Tide Vivid with the chlorine-free bleach on the wind. It was the smell of tennis and summer at the shore, and Farah even thought that she could hear the swoosh of the ocean trailing off behind him, the squeals of frolicking children.

"So, then, what do you think? Will Joanne like it?"
"Sorry . . . ?"
"I don't want her to think I'm some kind of degenerate . . . I'm sorry, but what was your name again?"
"Farah," she replied. "But call me 'Fah.'" Then, while he was already lying at her feet, and the wool of his sweater was

becoming increasingly blood-soaked, she thought how stupid it was to introduce herself to someone she was just then shooting; it was a good thing she had had the presence of mind not to give her last name.

She covered his body, well, as well as she could, with her *Yogalife,* and, pulling up her pajamas, whose legs had already become saturated with the flowing blood, she walked away toward the ocean, which roared in the distance—eternal, boundless, understanding.

CHAPTER 2

It was Friday; that same night, Joanne had dreamed she was having sexual relations with the delivery guy from BBQueen Grill. He was a short, uncomely Mexican with a wild look and work-worn, definitely brutality-capable hands whose touch disgusted her with the whole of her being, but which she also visibly desired. Because now, as he, having tossed the thermal-insulated bag with her beloved chicken wings into the foyer, was raping her, she, though resisting, was doing so without conviction, and at the same time all of this was giving her, as happens, a sensual pleasure that was hard to deny.

Suddenly she heard a gunshot. Obviously that happens in this city, full of weirdos; everyone who lives here, when he hears a shot, immediately starts yawning, because he knows it by heart: the ambulance, the flashing lights, the gawkers shrugging their shoulders, and the cops who, besides scattering greasy donut wrappers everywhere, "are not releasing any information."

Joanne shoved her lover aside like a sack of dry leaves, then opened the door and . . .

The white-ruffed alley cat was lying there motionless, like it was sleeping. *What kind of sick monster would shoot an innocent cat?* Joanne thought, taking her phone out to call the police. Once she had gotten closer to it, however, she understood that a cat's all well and good, but there was some person there, too. A magazine had been draped quite casually over him, and he was ringed in an expanding puddle of blood.

She stared vacantly at the tracks of smallish, bloody feet, which "left" the room, led down the stairs, out the entryway, turned left on Water Street, and headed north, toward the ocean.

"It's obvious!" she whispered, marveling at her own ingenuity. "He was killed by someone without shoes!"

This discovery totally exhausted her newly discovered detective skills, and Joanne carefully lifted the magazine from his face . . .

It was, to her pleasant shock, a new *Yogalife*! Was this some bonus issue?

It happened to be opened to a personality test, already filled out a little, something along the lines of "Is Yoga Your Whole Life?" or "Are You a Sexy Yogi?" She perched herself tout de suite beside the body of Frank from yoga, the one who sometimes looked at her so strangely, and, leaning against his savagely bullet-riddled corpse, she started taking the personality test with great passion, blood sloshing over her pecked-at stilettos all the while.

When she was telling them about this dream at work the following day, she completely skipped the part about the BBQueen delivery guy, but she delighted in analyzing the stuff about the cat, the corpse, and the bloody footprints. It was collectively determined that it was all "totally Lynch," and that someone should write a screenplay about it, but Joanne, returning home in her preposterous Ford Pinto, was already thinking—though it goes without saying it's not a done deal—about what she would do with the ten million dollars she'd get for the rights, that it would be enough for everything she ever wanted.

CHAPTER 3

When Farah and Joanne first met . . . It was April, or May even, hard to say now, though you could definitely nail it down going by their text messages . . . They hit it off fatally right from the get-go, and they talked all evening, walking intently up and down Royal Barber Street, totally incapable of parting ("And you get it, she had on this blue velour dress, anyway, velour wears out fast." "Speaking of blue, these blue sweats I've been wearing lately when I drive to yoga . . ." "Get out of town, I always walk to yoga." "I like walking in general, but with a quick, springy step, never slowly." "My nephew is very slow. I swear you've never seen a more sluggish shithead." "My nephew eats everything with ketchup. Can you imagine? He'll eat his cornflakes with ketchup if you don't catch him in time!"). And however many times it seemed they'd run out of things to talk about and that there was nothing left to add, they would turn right around and find a lot to latch onto, no problem, something always occurred to one or the other ("Unfortunately, ketchup is *totally* carcinogenic." "Speaking of which, my Aunt Albie has bone cancer." "Oh, the poor thing! That must really hurt." "It's a good thing she's religious. Studies say that religious people are better at handling pain. Would you like some antibacterial gel?" "Sure, a little, thanks. Though I feel sorry for the bacteria. They're living creatures. I know that sometimes I sound like a nut." "No, why? It's your right to think that." "It's because of my Buddhism—it's completely changed my point of view."), and there was nothing to suggest that things would someday take the turn they did.

The evening city was seething in its basin like black soup garnished with glass and light, bubbling over with secrets and excess; dogs barked, the subway wailed, someone who'd been raped or had merely had her handbag snatched was screaming horribly in the distance, and artificial fires flared into the darkness over the river, promising that, still, anything could happen.

Oh, you need to know what Joanne looked like, objectively, and then you'll get the paradox of the situation for yourself. Anyway, you might have seen her a few times before, since she worked at the salon by the subway entrance on Bohemian Street, the one next to Chase. You've probably caught a flash of her face, with its rather fleshy mouth and cheeks like currants, an alabaster face rounded like a doll's and with makeup to match, all protruding lashes and meaningfully upturned eyes, with hair the color of artificial chestnut lacquered to the point of perfect imperviousness to the most severe weather conditions. She was always dressed according to a formula known only to her, something like "comfortable yet ugly, with a hint of extravagance," masking her assets by excessively exposing what didn't call for it. She avoided cotton, jeans, and other symptoms of textile banality, reserving particular esteem for stunning creations whose operatic lace puffed out like fire retardant over her abundant bosom; their ordinary uncommonness would "break through," first with their classical elegance, then with their athletic motifs, and ultimately giving off the

11

appearance of a Russian girl coming home from New Year's every day of her life.

No, Joanne was certainly not very attractive.

That's what Fah thought, and she also thought that hers was unfortunately an objective opinion. Jo had thin legs and always wore ragged stilettos with heels that had been plucked off and decentered like they were cross-eyed, and that she notoriously painted with nail polish; this unstable load-bearing construction nearly buckled under her substantial corpus. Her head had been planted directly onto her shoulders, as if the Creator had felt like using her person to test whether the invention of the neck had not been an entirely accidental occurrence.

So, should you desire to examine it, it would seem not to be there.

She had a low voice and laugh, the kind one usually hears at the crack of dawn in bars where sumo wrestlers are celebrating their triumphs alongside serial killers as the naked cross-eyed chicks and rough-hewn dragons are writhing in their secret travails up the latters' backs.

She wasn't interested in anything, and that was fine by her; she mostly listened to awful shopworn songs and would hum them off-key while cutting her clients' hair; she didn't know how to cook, and she'd watch whatever was on TV, didn't matter if it was *Blow-Up* or a documentary about rutting antelopes or a show about the lives of people who exercise on elliptical machines; she couldn't care less about a movie's title, its director, how it ended or how it began, she just took television in like a rapid stream of illusion in which she eagerly splashed without rhyme or reason. Which meant rarely, if she was using antibacterial gel.

"Jo, do you want some?" Fah asked.

"No thanks."

"But it's antibacterial gel."

"Oh . . . Thank you, but no."

"Jo?"

"It dries out my hands!"

"You have to use it."

"Fah, they're living creatures."

"Jo?! Did you see the guy who was holding on to the bar before we got on?"

(He was the type who doesn't wash his hands after he pees. Was Jo blind? He was the type who doesn't even unzip his fly to pee.)

"Fine, maybe a little."

Furthermore, she never had time for anything, because besides the salon on Bohemian she was always running pointlessly around with the totally wrong guys. Much of her attention was consumed by setting erotic snares, friending people on Facebook, scoring addresses and telephone numbers, sending risqué texts, arranging the perfect circumstances for her to bump into the current object of her affections with a mug of steaming-hot coffee, pouring most of it over herself, so that *summa summarum* most of her hours were spent nursing her scalded heart with whiskey on the rocks and puttying it back together with the huge rainbow-sprinkled muffins she bought at Loraz Markets.

Yes, perhaps she dreamed of love.

•

Though she maintained that it was quite the opposite. "Promise me something, Fah," she said one day as they were on their way to get coffee at that utterly trendy Bad Berry, where various oddballs sit out the livelong day, exposing the world to their exceptionality, the crux of which, it turns out later, is situated in their glasses frames . . . The coffee's coffee, no revelation tastewise, and Fah thought that she might be out of her mind to be paying eight dollars for a regular coffee. Out the window stretched a view onto dusty Bath, opalescent in the heat, full of commotion and afternoon bustle, of mothers with children and schlubby hipsters in alpine caps despite the heat, with bags that recalled old scrota. "Promise me something, Fah," Joanne said. "From now on we're done with ratty old boys, okay? No more boys, no more socks, no more sound of them scratching their balls in the sleepless night. Promise me. Death to douchebags!"

"Anyway, to be honest, I wonder whether I'm a lesbian. In the long run, when I think about it, there's something to it, don't you think?"

"Why aren't you saying anything? You never thought about being a lesbian? I think it's terribly sexy."

Is there really any point to saying what happened next? Almost immediately following these declarations, which, after all, had not originated with Farah, Joanne fell in love with a pathetic—yes, pathetic, in Fah's opinion—salesman at a kitchen and bath store, allegedly with a degree in Hungarian Studies but unable to find work in his field, we all know the drill. A scrawny sort of fellow, eternally entangled in the spiderweb of his own limbs, plus with a shiny little bald spot that he concealed obsessively beneath cunning strokes of his hairbrush. But a bald spot that, despite his efforts, was unruly and inquisitive, in its own way intelligent, and time and again would emerge like a sensation-greedy egg out of the fluffy, if sparse, hay of his hair, casting its cheerful flashes of light left and right.

Setting aside the oath she'd sworn to herself not half a second before, which, let us recall, had not originated with Fah . . . but come on . . . that bald spot . . . it could cave in. Joanne was obviously delighted and would turn up the volume whenever the radio played that moronic commercial for Tip-Tap Kitchen & Bath, where he worked ("For Tip-Tap faucets, get your faucets at Tip-Tap"), and she made everyone listen as she sank into utter bliss. But Fah thought all of this was at the same level of disgusting as their dates, she thought it revolting how this tapeworm would speculate or even dream on the topic of her friend's physicality, how squeezing her hand gingerly at the movies, running his fingers along her papillary lines, he would turn his thoughts, if only in his mind, to pressing against her body with his own . . . Several times, during their chance meetings, she'd caught the scent of his body. He smelled like a goat that's just brushed its teeth. But what pained and shamed her most was that while he was putting the moves on Jo, it was as if she, Fah, didn't exist, as if she were made of air.

Anyway, when it came to her, he wasn't convinced that she wasn't.

She wanted all this to be untrue, for it to turn out that Jo had misplaced her contact lenses, but as soon as she got the cash, oh yes, then she'd buy some new ones, she'd see the truth, and everything would return to normal. Again they'd go out for coffee, tittering at the sight of these super-hot guys coming out of Chase in their Hugo Boss sweaters, cramming their pockets with thousand-dollar bills for minor expenses . . . And waiting for them in the convertible just around the corner, the typical specimen of gap-toothed girl who, unburdened of the specter of defecation, weighs twenty kilos, in beige moccasins, a dress made of peach-colored paper, and guinea-pig embryo furs, refreshing herself on Perrier and a whiff of chocolate . . .

"Gosh, you don't think her name's Chloe, do you?" Jo asked with a sigh, gawking, despite her new contacts, in a manner that could hardly have been called discreet. "I could never be that skinny."

"Why not? You could."

"I like the wings at BBQueen Grill way too much. And Heath Bars. Heath Bars are better than orgasms."

Jo clearly took the coughing fit that erupted from Fah as encouragement to expand on the topic, for she immediately added:

"I love orgasms."

And then:

"It's this feeling of the utter impossibility that is gripping mankind. Of the impossibility of anything! . . . Hey, Farah, what do you think about that?"

What was impossible was that Joanne was saying such a thing! As if she wanted to add: "Oh, but you wouldn't know anything about that," or, "From now on I'm only going to use comparisons and references to things you're clueless about," or else simply, "But how would you know anything about that, after all, you're not . . . Oh, look over there!" "Where?" "Too late, Farah, too late. A pretty little bird just flew by."

What was impossible was the Hungarianist, what was impossible was the shiny egg of his skull, which Fah dreamed about night after night. She dreamed of Jo stamping passionate kisses all over it.

From that point on Fah boycotted him as much as she could. She polemicized against his views, even if he were to say, "That's a sidewalk," while pointing at the sidewalk; she programmatically refused to laugh at his jokes, the deference he showered on Jo made her want to throw up, his flourish when throwing his jacket over her shoulders, as if what he was wrapping her in had just been plucked from the sky, sort of like a little fry-scented cloud, and the fact that he lent her money for the subway ride home. She would raise her eyebrows meaningfully and stare at these two, who in her eyes truly appeared as substandard sperm sucking up to the egg.

Big deal, as God is her witness she would try to maintain a proper relationship, even as Jo stopped taking their meetings seriously. They were supposed to hang out at the mall all afternoon, the way they loved to, they could do it endlessly. They'd look over the mats at the local Yogamart, and then at the rain boots Jo dreamed of getting, the cash for which she always blew, only to lock themselves in the handicapped fitting room at H&M, which could accommodate two people squealing for a quarter hour at a time, whispering and trying on those fabulous little disposable sparkly-threaded sweaters that after a single wash transform into a set of very long, still-sparkly sleeves, which are then great for wrapping around you or for jump-rope or else for a tow cable or maybe . . .

("Honey, what do you think about this one?" "Oh my God, don't get that. It makes you look fat." "It's cute!" "It's awful." "Really?" "Bright colors make you look fat, darks are slimming." "It's the same little designs." "My mother was wearing a dress with a little pattern on the day I was born." "I was born at three in the morning. That's why I can stay up late, no problem." "I get up in the morning pretty much whenever." "You have no idea. I stay up late and in the morning I'm a total mess." "I get up in the morning." "In the morning I drink a ton of coffee, and then I'm all jitters. If it weren't for meditation, I'd be a bundle of nerves." "You want some gel?" "Thanks, maybe later.")

They could jabber on like this till evening, when, worn out, with mugs of decaf and skim milk and bags filled with their purchases, they'd part by the subway. But that was then. Now, several hours before that would have happened, the phone rang.

"It meant a lot to me that we were supposed to go out," Joanne was saying blithely, "but today I'm going out with . . ."

"I see." It was a good thing Fah knew how to conceal her disappointment with a long, meaningful pause, fanning herself with a bag of algae powder. "No biggie, I have a lot of work to do anyway. And besides, it's sick how hot it is. The movies in weather like this . . ."

"I know what you're saying. Fortunately, the IMAX is air-conditioned."

"Jo, with all due respect, you're well aware how much crap there is in air-conditioned spaces. And the soundproof panels . . . Gross. They reek like dirty socks!"

"Can I help it if I feel like the fucking movies? The dark, a Coke, popcorn . . ."

Dead silence.

"Fah?"

"Sorry, Jo, I got lost in thought."

"But you know, you could . . ."

"No, no, absolutely not, I brought all this paperwork home."

"Well, have it your way."

"It's a great idea, I'd love to, but I have a lot to do."

"In that case, I won't press you."

"I'd like to go with you . . . I mean, the two of you, but you understand."

"Maybe it's for the best: it's a long time since we've gone somewhere just the two of us."

But since they had been so insistent . . . Not wanting to disappoint them, she finally ended up going with them to an evening show at the IMAX. Let stupid excuses be someone else's specialty. In the strange, muffled slurping and heavy breathing coming from the darkness nearby, she suspected neither the insertion of tongue into ear, nor the fumbling of a finger in Joanne's labia—done, it so happens, rather inexpertly. Having thoroughly disinfected her hands, she was following the film with grim diligence, one of those incomprehensible European gloomfests where everyone looks at each other for a long time, only in the end to suddenly say "ecstasy" as the camera follows a floating shopping bag. What's worse, it was she who'd insisted that they see this instead of *Die Really Quite Hard 134* or the latest sequel to *Fatal Menstruation,* and they didn't much care.

Now she was vindictively imagining what she would tell them if they wanted her to let them know what they'd missed while they were lost in their game of snap-the-elastic in each other's underwear.

The worst part was that they didn't even ask her about it afterward. For Farah, the only faint consolation she'd have from this nightmare would be counting the calories (as well as the bacteria) that, in her eyes, Jo would then absorb with the Coke (unwashed hands), the double whiskey on the rocks, and the gigantic gyro (and she a vegetarian!), and all at so late an hour that she wouldn't burn any of it off.

"As far as I'm concerned," she said with her mouth full, "right now we're gobbling up those off-navy Hunter boots I've been dreaming about. I'm maybe eating the sole. You?"

"I'm eating the lining," said the Hungarianist.

"Jo, don't laugh," Fah burst out, "but eating after six is one of the main causes of obesity."

"Not if they're rain boots."

"That's right, they're supposed to be good for you."

"They're high in vitamin Cal."

"And vitamin Lo."

"And they're lo-cal-oric."

"Localrainic!"

"I think vitamin Lo might be bad for your brain," she could have said to Joanne, who was tittering at her own moldering jokes. Or simply hurled her gyro at the Hungarianist in his tacky palm-tree-patterned shirt, from whose open collar curled sparse, dark ringlets of hair. Only instead she looked away. It was an utterly ordinary snack bar, plus they were laughing loudly the whole time, their attention turned only to each other. They threw coins into the jukebox and sang off-key to the hits of that fat-as-a-barrel Beyoncé. "Let's drive to the ocean . . ." he whispered (". . . just as soon as I plug the earphones into my Walkman," Fah completed the sentence in her mind), "whenever you want to, Jo."

"Don't forget your eyes!" Fah could have said to her then, as she herself was getting out in Bath and they were driving off into a night filled with kisses, caresses, and liquor spilling all over faded Snoopy sheets. "Despite appearances, they sometimes come in handy!"

But this comeback occurred to her only later, after many hours of obsessive brooding over their salivary exploits, distasteful gestures, constant rubbing, kneading, clinging, pawing, the shenanigans they got into deliberately, as if wanting to tell her, "Don't take it the wrong way, Fah, but this has nothing to do with you."

And thus whiling away her time contemplating stinging retorts that would come off as impartial remarks elaborately laced with venom—the wittier they were, the less likely they were ever to be said aloud—she overlooked when that change that was so hard not to notice had occurred in Joanne, in her personal chemistry.

•

It was sort of like . . . As if the summer nights spent with the Hungarianist/shop clerk in the small, tasteless, wood-paneled apartment that Jo rented on the river . . . as if those nights when her screams fell from the windows into the courtyard on one side, into Water Street on the other, and crashed against the asphalt and the walls of the neighboring buildings like jettisoned potted plants, as if they had pitted her, had bored her clean of what she'd once contained.

As if the mouth, hands, and stinger of that moderately attractive man, who in this whole ceremony figured more as an extra, a third-rate altar boy rather than the priest, had exorcised the old Jo, unsure of herself, her cross-toed heels flying after some dipshits in her porcine trot. After which they stuffed her insides with a completely different sub-stance, jams that were super-sweet, nutritious, and impres-sively high-calorie (calorainy) (*ha ha ha!*).

Now she was more prone to roll her eyes, she wore greasy, flag-red lipstick, ironed her hair straight, so that it looked fake, and every morning, first smearing her legs in moisturizer until they shined like glass, she would run a pencil straight up to her butt, so that under the appropriate shade of stockings it would look like a seam.

The aura of erotic greed, the kind that is sated wil-ly-nilly, radiated from Joanne and drew looks that Farah initially attributed to her friend's funny attire, but anyone nearby knew the nature of the electromagnetic poles that arose wherever she showed up. Store clerks left their regis-ters, baristas stopped making espresso, insurance salesmen set aside their policies and allowed them to be lifted by the wind and carried over the city unfilled, unsigned, and unprofitable, and she stood there, smelling sweetly of sweat, shawarma, lipstick, the several different perfumes she'd quickly sprayed on herself at Sephora, hair spray, and hot love, with its intrinsic note, it so happens, of urine.

Anyway, let's leave off Jo already, for God's sake. When it comes down it, she's a nice, mentally strong, jolly good lass, and it would be a shame if you were to see her exclusively through the prism of her erotic magnetism. Jo loves to joke; she has a really cool, husky laugh; anyone who knows hairdressery knows that she's great at her job. But even that handsome Frank from yoga, and by his smart getup and healthy skin you could count on him for a modicum of taste, followed her with his eyes when she once drove up to the school in her idiotic Ford Pinto and got out to pull the leaves off her wipers.

(Though we can't be sure that she did so out of common concern. Jo was wearing cowboy boots and that tight dress in the fattening seafaring design, which swathed her ample bosom and ass in a tangle of roses, anchors, and chains. In it she looked like a hard-pickled ham pimped out with legs.)

In the silence, in their increasingly rare encounters and polite phone calls, a kind of grudge had grown between them. The asymmetry of their priorities, outlooks on life, aesthetic conventions, their attitude toward life. What had been similar had flitted elsewhere, had faded to the wings and given way to what was no longer simply "just different," but totally opposite, irreconcilable, and in fact altogether

23

mutually exclusive. The situation came to a head during a telephone conversation that changed everything.

"I'm not going to yoga, I feel awful," Jo said, though you could hear the excitation in her voice.

"Maybe it's parasites?" Fah suggested, sensing that it wasn't that at all. "They say there's this Mongolian doctor who sees patients on Royal Barber . . . All the girls from work go to see him. He supposedly probes you with something that looks like a ski pole. I was thinking, 'Maybe it just is a ski pole, Ingeborg.' But I didn't want to say that to her. She'd shelled out two hundred dollars for some turbo-reaming and another hundred for . . ."

"It's not that, I'm just worried that we . . ." Jo said. "You know . . ."

"What the hell are you saying?" Fah whispered. "What's that mean?" she added more loudly, making a show of her great freedom, and then added an extra "Heh heh" just in case there was any doubt as to whether she was *really* free, or merely free.

Jo slurped nonchalantly, and you could hear her opening a jar of peanut butter.

"I don't know, I could be . . ."

"Yes?"

"I forgot to take my last couple of pills. That is, I remembered, but it was already late at night."

Fah didn't hear what Jo said after that: she was so shocked that to buy herself some time she grabbed the *Yogalife* from the table and started crumpling its pages into the receiver, and then—having yanked the line a bit, at the same time repeating "Jo, I can hardly hear you! Hey, you're breaking up!"—she put the receiver down, and to complete the effect she disconnected the phone and spent the next long while quivering.

24

•

The fact that they . . . they were . . . with each other . . .

While she . . .

Of course she'd suspected—boy, did she ever suspect!
Yet it was only now that it hit her explicitly, in all clarity, and
with a painful slap, as if someone had struck her cheek. She
still couldn't come out and say it, she couldn't provide the
reasons, but she felt that she'd been defeated on all fronts, or
rather that . . .

The greatest perfidy was that she didn't even have rational arguments, appropriate words . . . *What else could I have
expected?* she asked herself dully, smoking, or rather pacing her
apartment dramatically with the cigarette she'd found in the
sideboard when she moved here. She chalked up her distress to
concern. Joanne was completely irrational; the wee thing was
hurtling toward disaster. "Have you gotten tested for HI . . . ?"
—no, no, no, she immediately deleted that text—watch yourself, Fah! After all, she had no right to be honest about what
she was thinking; the most she could do was maybe eke out
some clichés: "It'll all work out, Jo," "Chin up," etc.

Especially given the fact that he was clearly turning her
against Farah, he would interpret her every gesture back-
ward! She saw how he looked at her, as if he were thinking,
*Take out that gel one more time and I'll take you to the nuthouse
myself!*

Anyway, that wasn't the point, it didn't even matter that
Joanne was doing it.

•

The perfidy was that she was doing it while Farah was not.

As absurd as that sounds!

She was hurt by it, especially given that in the last issue of *Yogalife* there had been a huge article about the health aspects of copulation (oxygenation, restoration of equilibrium to one's energies, burning calories). And here someone as carefree and incapable of order as Joanne was suddenly extracting all the benefits of sex that Farah could obtain only through minute Sisyphean efforts.

She could now literally hear their sniggering, which showed that Jo felt no sense of loyalty whatsoever. Even if they hadn't meant anything by it—as they now happened to be trying to explain, "the poor thing is going crazy, she really has to get out and find someone . . ." She literally heard it, as if they had said it in front of her, not realizing that she was right there, and she pictured them suddenly turning around as she's standing at the door . . .

And they go on: "It's not like that, Farah, wait! We didn't mean anything by it!" But now she's running away, biting her lip from the pain till it bleeds . . . It's pouring rain, the passersby in ponchos step aside as she runs down the street coughing, howling with pain, betrayed, cheated, not having sex!

Perhaps it was precisely this dramatic vision that sort of inspired her that very evening, ordering those off-navy Hunter rain boots on eBay—the very ones that Jo had been dreaming of but was never able to pull together the cash for.

•

That and digging the birth control pills out of the medicine cabinet, the ones she took two years ago for acne. Now she would always be sure to have them spill out of her bag at key moments on a wave of bottles of antibacterial gel. Then she could stuff them back in with that exasperation that is typical of children chastising their imaginary friends.

Now, she was looking at the cigarette held between her fingers, and she felt a rather unexpected, yet irresistible desire to extinguish it on herself, in her own palm. The sudden desire for physical pain, in which everything could burn out, dissolve, was so intense that it terrified her. She jabbed at the surface of the wi   ndow and observed as the cigarette, still burning, flew into an urban night full of lights and speeding taxis. Spinning, it drops down, down, along with her illusions, her feelings, and everything.

Like an itty-bitty burning ballerina.

Like a shard of a Christmas star smashed by hoodlums.

CHAPTER 4

Anyway, that's pretty typical, it often happens like that.

Totally unlike men, those who are in love with their pastimes, their contests, warriors of all manner of "mine is better," women adore a round of "I have the same one." Running into each other, they manage to while away the days and nights and reassure themselves as to the twin-like similarity of their experiences and travails; even their physiology delectates in sisterly affinities, synchronizing their monthly cycles. Then they sip flavored coffees and marvel at the infinitude of miraculous parallelisms in their traumas, tastes in movies, and favorite foods; they want to divvy up their failures, their triumphs, and their downward spirals fairly. "If you love me, you have the same thing," they declare to each other in this mute oath of undying empatho-symmetry. They make up facts, adjust the details, keep quiet about the differences, tailor their memories; they speak one language, so that after a couple of weeks of preparing all the proofs of their twin-ness they believe in it themselves.

In twos, things go swimmingly!

But just wait until one of them says, "Mine is totally different," or, "I don't really like goat cheese." Wait till she raises a hand against that sweet symbiosis, an idyllic, programmatic unity smelling of face powder and Orbit gum. That will cut off the procession of empathy, it will tear the Siamese sisters apart like an expired coupon. Just wait until one of them suddenly gets married while the other stays single, just wait till one of them starts voting for the right wing, whereas the other is for the liberals, and this masterful, albeit flimsy, construction will collapse into malevolent trembling, so as to fold, often in the course of just a few moments, like a house of cards, the one good thing being that no one ever lived there.

"Whoops, false alarm :)" Jo texted not long after. But Farah just gave a vacant snort. She had sort of been waiting for the occasion, which had to arrive, of the invitation, for the attempted contact that she could spitefully refuse, shove away with disgust, like a dish she'd once thought divine that *she no longer had a taste for.* And now that time had come.

Though it gave her significantly less pleasure than she had expected. It was just then that she started to get down in the dumps, under mounds of loneliness. The unfathomed vault of emptiness from which she drew gray gems of crushing loneliness, necklaces of suspended silence, reams of dusky hours.

She would return from work, tossing the sad Styrofoam meal on the table. Biobean, which a short time ago had looked quite convincing behind the freezer door in the deli section at Loraz, once Farah had purchased it and brought to her apartment went imperceptibly cold, limp, and spoiled, so that when she opened it, it turned out to be an apathetic blot of Play-Doh-flavored muck. Organic meals, whose packaging presented the juicy breasts of happy chickens and colorful bouquets of nitrate-free vegetables, turned out when heated to be a steaming illustration of the saying that a person wants to "eat his cake and have it too": they looked exactly as though they'd already been eaten by somebody and, despite this, were still lying on the plate, and on top of that Farah didn't want them at all.

She brought the groceries in. She took the trash out. The sun, fiercely yellow from the haze of the Indian restaurant, fell through her busted shades. There was a distinct possibility that she was slowly turning into curry, but she wasn't even close enough with anyone at work for him to tell it to her straight when it had happened. And as far as yoga was concerned, well . . .

"Hey . . . I'm sorry, what was your name?" he said to her one Wednesday—Frank, the one she liked so much.

"Farah," Farah said. "But call me 'Fah.'"

She tried to smile, but all she could see was the *Yogalife* covering his face.

"I dreamt of you . . . In a strange way."

"Really?" Fah asked, flushing red all over.

"It's not what you think . . . I mean . . ."

"Don't sweat it. I sometimes dream up unbelievable nonsense too."

"No, no, it's not that."

"Maybe it's the full moon?"

Some kind of unpleasant tension reigned between them.

"Apropos your friend . . . ?"

"Yeah?"

"The one . . . What's her name?"

"I don't know which one you're talking about."

"I thought you came here together with . . ."

"Joanne?" Farah yielded.

"That's her. She doesn't come on Wednesdays anymore?"

"No," she burst into laughter. "She was having some issues: it looked like she might be pregnant."

"Oh my God!" he said. "Congratulations."

"But she's taken care of it."

His face expressed a confusion that Fah didn't feel like dispelling.

"Say hi to her from . . . Or better not. She won't know who you're talking about."

"I'm sure she will!"

. . . she stopped going to the classes. She would check her phone's dead screen a dozen times an hour. As though she had some pretext to expect a message with a confession of love, marriage proposals, a positive pregnancy test and the due date. What she did get was mail to the effect that she had won, which turned out to be information about the possibility of winning, and a newsletter for Jehovah's Witnesses, but when she wanted to throw it into the garbage the people staring at her from its pages were so smiley, were so decent and clean-cut, that for a while she thought that, in her current situation, not joining them would be a tactical error she wouldn't be able to forgive herself for someday.

Besides that, she didn't receive much correspondence, not counting, of course, ads for breast enlargement. As far as that was concerned, there is no way she could forget that the opportunity was always there.

("Breast enlargement!" they were constantly writing to her, despite her never writing back.)

("Penis enlargement and scrotal lengthening!")

31

("Free brain reduction with every enlargement (penis or both breasts).")

("Brain reduction! Are you thinking too much? Remembering too much? Mulling too much over? Are you wondering why you've endured so much suffering? Brain reduction will free you from these troubles.")

("Reduce your brain, you'll be all smiles and will truly enjoy life!")

("Hurry, sale ends soon: *no fear of death!* With every brain removal, we'll remove your fear for free.")

("Help the Sahara! We earmark 0.00001% of our clinic's proceeds to save the desert's natural beauty!★")

(★by not going there for vacation, because it's such a clusterfuck)

She tried to make friends at work, she even went to karaoke, but she left after half an hour.

They were constantly talking about who wrote what on Twitter, who read what on Facebook, and who invited whom to what. One could assume that that's why she was sitting off to the side the whole time, pretending to be drinking her hot sake and chopping a grain of sushi rice in half with her fork. Upon returning home, she set up the appropriate account and awaited a change of luck, and by the following day something like that had already occurred: she got an invitation from Steve, her middle school boyfriend, to join his circle of friends. She closed the site and never logged in again. She set up her profile on a dating service (we guarantee a good date!), but besides filling out the humiliatingly idiotic questionnaire ("for you, love means . . . ," "as far as food goes, your absolute 'I'll-always-eat-it' is . . . ," etc.) they required her to send a photo; besides, it was true what she said—she wasn't messing around, and no one wrote to her anyway.

Ultimately—it was the dreams that were finishing her off.

Whole nights long she was now dreaming these sexual odysseys in which relatives she'd only ever seen once were hooking up in twos or threes with friends from grade school or counselors from summer camp, and they paraded before her like this until dawn, extremely proud of the preposterousness of the configurations they'd assumed. Somewhere nearby she heard the sea crashing against the cliffs, and it suddenly occurred to her that her Aunt Albie; Steven, her boyfriend from high school; the trainer from her gym; her yoga instructor; Ingeborg, who worked at the reception desk; Joanne—they'd all been perfect friends for years, though they'd never mentioned it to her! Now they were flaunting their intimacy ostentatiously before her; they performed demonstrative gestures, grabbed each other by the arm in showy alliances, as if they'd wanted to throw it in her face that "what could you know about it, Fah, you've never had a head for this!"

Before she'd managed to riffle through her thoughts for secrets that one could pass along to the other, it turned out that they were all already being circulated. They were showing each other the pictures of her in the bath with her cousin, her Google search history, they were commenting on the fact that she repeatedly visited sites about athlete's foot and parasitic diseases (wonder why!), they even dragged out the mattress from the loft in her summer house, which she had stained with menstrual blood. They played dodgeball with her dirty stockings, and in Monopoly she got stuck with a worn pumice stone as a die (hee hee hee, Farah rolled a five!), they tried playing with the dead cat lying in the street in front of her building.

"You're getting polyps, Fah, I can hear it," her mother told her. "But the reason I'm calling is Aunt Albie had a dream about you."

"Aunt Albie?!"

"Twice, even! She called from Prixton specifically to tell me about it."

"But she has bone cancer." Farah decided to play for time.

"That has nothing to do with it. It really upset her. She dreamt you were walking in your pajamas with the legs all blood-spattered."

"It's not true!"

"She asked me if you're seeing someone."

"Mooooom."

"Let me finish! Her friend, who reads tarot, said it's possible you'll meet someone soon."

"I have met someone," Farah retorted, only to change the subject.

"Is it a man?"

"Yes."

"That's good, at least. You don't know what a weight that is off my shoulders. You're sure that . . ."

"I don't think so, Mom."

"Dear, if you sense that he's a drinker, break it off right away. At your age you already have too much to lose, and a relationship with someone who likes to get drunk is going to come back on you no matter how you cut it, it doesn't

matter how much he might have charmed you and showered you with compliments. You deserve someone who
respects you, you've always had such lovely hair!"

It was true that she'd met somebody.
At least, it wasn't entirely untrue.

CHAPTER 5

A Life Filled with Miracles: Learn to See the Magic of Existence in Just 14 Days, by Manfred Peterson, Ph.D., 134 pages, hardcover. Can I tell you something honestly about this book? My mother read it, too, when my father left her with the mortgage, a dog dying of cancer, and a bad fucking case of thickening eyelashes, while he ran off with a nineteen-year-old. She couldn't deal with the unpleasant feelings that came with constantly running into them at Wal-Mart.

"I can't look at it," she would sob into the phone to her friends in the evening. "Like it's nothing, the little girl sits in the shopping cart between bags of cornflakes, and Jack, picking up speed, leaps onto its goddamn frame and slaloms between the shelves of bread and pyramid-stacked cans of chowder!" You could pour out the tears with a bucket. "I can still hear it ringing in my ears, him screaming 'Yabba dabba dooo!' to the whole Wal-Mart! There was nothing security could do about it!"

"He never gave ME a ride like that!!!"

This depression lasted up until she actually read *A Life Filled with Miracles* and utterly freed herself from negative emotions and habitual hang-ups. And though I can't really say for sure that it was she who left this book in the laundry room of the building where Fah lived, willing this godsend of reinvigoration to go forth into the world, it was an absolutely certain fact that one day, on the way back with her laundry, Farah found it.

From the author's words it came to light that she was surrounded by thousands of miracles that she generally didn't notice, whereas "it's enough to stick out your hands and grab them by the fistful," "breathe your toxic emotions away," "become aware of how many chances you miss out on every day," "contempt blocks you off from what really matters," "whether it's a fluffy muffin, a dog full of life, or a gab session with an older lady out on a stroll."

She resolved unequivocally to open herself to the richness of existence and to enjoy every moment. She even started to experience something similar to hope, of the most mediocre variety: for whatevs.

She resolved to make new friends.

They'd get together, have pillow fights, and accompany each other through their daily defeats.

She didn't have to wait long for the effects of the changes that had occurred within her. It turned out that she was doing her laundry on the exact same evening as her first-floor neighbor.

He was a pale boy, bloated and translucent like marzipan, dressed in a black T-shirt with a print of some tangle of skulls and people fleeing aflame. His eyes, like skimpily apportioned trail mix, loomed somewhere deep in the dough of his face; and that, smeared with grease, edged by a few symbolic long hairs, expressed a great desire to bury itself in a pillow and wake up after many, many millions of years, only after it'd all be over.

"These fucking washing machines, they're destroying my clothes," he noted in a monotone, like someone talking in his sleep. A Pollyanna would maybe take this for a conversation-starter.

We might wonder whether she'd be so wise if she existed.

"You have Darth Vader underpants, that's funny," Farah noted with something that she would have wanted to be freedom, adjusting her hair. Her hair had always been her strong suit—by which one could also judge that a consistent diet and regular exercise, that all of it provides beneficial stimulation to the body and its natural resources.

Her attention clearly aroused his suspicion.

"And why exactly do you find that funny?"

"My nephew, he's a big fan as well. And anyway . . . How's it going?"

And why exactly had she asked that? He had bags under his eyes, a lovely couple of kilocalories he was saving for a rainy day, mainly around his moobs, and eyes as sharp as those of someone who's spent these last twenty years drowned in a pond.

"Yes, I'm very happy, no doubt," he said, not so much joyfully as blithely, with the nonchalance of a Satanist.

Fah was holding her greyish bra from H&M.

He answered her that he'd played his fair share of *Counterstrike* online and hadn't slept much, maybe hardly at all. And then they'd found him in the entryway, towel-clad, globs of soapy foam under his armpits, trembling on the floor-mat. He stated that while he was taking a shower his uncle barged in on him, it seriously pissed him off, and he couldn't be convinced to come back in. To this day he's pretty much against entering anywhere, though his real problem is exiting.

Both his monthlong stay in a locked ward and all that therapeutic yada yada for the wackos, "point to your hatred for your mother and color it in"—in his case they weren't worth the shit they were smeared with.

Why not? Maybe because he was normal, that's all. And then that last doctor, anyway, in his opinion, he was pretty fucked up himself, so he should know what he's talking about, he would measure out the doses of Bordax and Cheezequakinium, which before had merely made him sleepy, so that he could snooze for dozens of hours on end . . .

". . . it achieved the desired result. Yeah, I don't know if you've ever tried Kidstainium. I don't know what it did for you, but it totally wakes me right back up. I'm so awake I can't do anything, I'm aware of everything and notice too many aspects of the one problem I'd like to bring up, talk over, fix, discuss, or at the least give the apartment a thorough vacuuming and clean the blinds with an old toothbrush. Anyway, when the situation overloads my senses past what I can stand, I take a Cheezequakinium and half a Bordax, which settles me down completely: then I totally know that nothing's going to happen if I don't do any of these things. I have everything under complete control. I achieve a perfect state of mental balance, a state you'd really like to find your-self in. People spend years meditating just to get close."

"What state is that?" Farah asks, because she's open, ready to take in life's miracles, and she doesn't break off conversations just like that, just because he, having already burned all his photos and documents, feels an urge to flee.

"It's a state of total consciousness and, at the same time, of total peace. I know everything I'm supposed to do at any given moment, being aware all the while how those things are ultimately nonsense, and that my chaotic struggles make no difference here . . . I go on, filling up this time with almost irrelevant activities, which allow me to shorten it."

"That's really cool," Farah said. "I'd say I sometimes have something like that when I take Theraflu for sinuses . . ."

"Were you doing something with blood?" he suddenly asked, looking around vigilantly.

Farah froze, her pajama bottoms in her hand.

"Pardon?" she mumbled.

A brick-red, scalding blush crept out from her neckline and gradually annexed her face.

"Sorry. I was just thinking."

"You were thinking that . . . ?"

"I always rinse blood in cold water before putting it in the wash."

"Really?"

"These fucked-up machines switch out your proper clothes for crap. You don't even know what happened with my Saddam Hussein shirt . . ."

Farah asked no further. For the next week she wouldn't go down to the laundry at all, and she was careful taking out the trash. The most important thing, however, was that the transformation now rising within her was more and more distinct, more and more overwhelming. Yes, it required time and patience; the gradual discovery of the joy of life is a long-term process full of conscious effort and an appropriate channeling of energy. Above all there was somehow no way to anticipate the changes in her old garments; Farah now spent huge amounts of time wandering around the mall and buying whatever, as though she were assembling a layette for her new self. She would fantasize about them meeting by chance someday, somewhere downtown, and Joanne wouldn't even recognize her. There'd be nary a trace of the old, good-natured, always-letting-herself-get-shoved-into-a-corner Fah, out of whom you could really make yourself a wonderful doormat, or else attach her to your ride like a fifth wheel and watch her bounce! An utterly altered woman would stand in her place, aware of her own value and transformation, encircled by a small group of crazed friends. Each would represent some particular "psychiatric type," would have a particular, delightful mania and style of dressing, and they'd have pillow fights, and . . .

What a paradox that it was on one of those very afternoons when, muttering to herself, she was leaning over a bin of discounted bras, she was enfolded in the specific, familiar fragrance of randomly selected perfumes and raw cabbage munched with Mentos and . . .

"Farah, is that you?! I didn't even recognize you," she suddenly heard, and she understood that it had already happened, and no attempts at sinking by sheer force of will even deeper into the earth had any chance of success now.

CHAPTER 6

Speaking of Bohemian Street, where Joanne worked, you ever hang out there?

It's a pleasant neighborhood pulsating with illicit life, a peculiar microcosm rich in sociological cacophony. Not quite able to concentrate on writing, at odds with the entire world, I've taken the subway there plenty of times, just to breathe the air, to take in a bit of the action, and go back home humming, *I have a lot of nothing . . . La la la . . . Nothing's just fine for me.* Bohemian has never disappointed me on this score. I could always count on an old hamburger getting stuck to my shoe, and that by the soup kitchen I'd be accosted by some big leathery black guy talking to himself and wearing a not-*très*-fresh Santa Claus cap.

"What's a sweet piece of ass like you doing here alone?" he'd call after every old lady teetering through the urban jungle, innocent as a lamb, with her wobbly walker. "Where's your fiancé, huh? He leave you, he promise and not show? Make a date with this old bastard, and I'll give it to you like a fella who knows how it's done!"

In his pants, which at the same time served him as a bag, and perhaps even a home, a rapscallion such as this typically keeps banana peels, VHS parts, and sometimes even feces, which could always come in handy later. These trousers are so dirty they're now waterproof—if not bulletproof! They're 100 percent organic, and you could probably teach them to respond to tone of voice or lead the blind across the roadway . . . You could easily offer the patent to North Face or Quechua. But trust me, he prefers his desperate lifestyle.

Yeah, you meet all kinds here, priest and pauper both. And Emperor No-Clothes, what with one of those nutty designers just having announced that the most fashionable getups this season are sewn out of air . . .

Light, somewhat diaphanous, ultrasexy, but the main thing is that they don't need to be washed . . . The downside: they're not so good at covering up the deficiencies of one's figure. That, and other people are breathing your clothes. On one corner, someone is pressing you with hip-hop recorded in the john at McDonald's, or else an original "Chenel" handbag, though the sack it's packed in looks like a better value for the four bucks they're asking. On another, a legless wino convinces you to surrender your life to Jesus and your money to him, because there's no profit in being a prophet . . . And right then, on the third corner, in a boutique hotel, on a golden sofa, beneath paintings by Kyovebgir Anogiv, who happens to be fetching ridiculous prices these days, the daughters of senators and various VIPs are sitting and drinking themselves stupid like it's no big thing, looking out over "All this disgustingly rich pussy" . . .

"What's Best for Throwing at a Plasma TV? We Test Champagne Glasses."

"Look Hot Five Minutes after an Abortion? It's Possible. Makeup Paramedics."

"Sexy in Detox. Ten Tricks for Looking like a Million Bucks When You Feel like Fifteen Old Deutschmarks."

"Daddy, I Crashed the Helicopter! Making the Most of an Amusing Slipup."

"Did You Know that Dogs are Mammals?! Interesting Science Facts."

You can't say, like, maybe these young folks don't have a knack for science, but when it comes to fashion they really know their stuff. Just take a look at the latest Zach de Boom collection they're wearing, called "Holy"—you can guess why. "Little Pilgrim Girl," she's the one inseminating the imaginations of the designers this season. Louboutin has put out a series of brain-twisted pumps inspired by nonpinching orthopedic sandals, and Vivienne Westwood says they go great with thick white tube socks with an emblem of crossed tennis rackets at the ankle, or else just bare feet covered in leprosy and bound in a checkered handkerchief. This season, hair is supposed to be unwashed, "unattractive"; obligatory: makeup that "gets greasy," dry lips (if at all possible, swollen from kissing a crucifix), slight self-mutilation. From a distance you'd think these are some crazy-ass chicks who've crawled here on their knees from Lourdes to announce the word of Christ, but, when you look a little closer, from between their polyester lips you see pearly teeth worth more than your soul, nay, than your entire shitty existence.

Now it seems to you that their sole occupation is screaming "Oh my God! Oh my God!" and looking around to see whether the great impression they're making is spread evenly across this vale of tears. But just try to drag yourself over to them, like a bag of trash that nobody needs—don't count on their pity: they'll eat you alive. First they'll say that, since you don't have bread, you should eat cake, and then that, since you don't have cake, you should eat cream pie with organic raspberries. "I don't have any pie like that," you whisper, painfully swallowing your saliva. "So tell them to jet you some from Switzerland." If there's one thing they despise, it's learned helplessness: no one ever coddled them, either. They, too, were once without a home, but did they moan about it? No, they bought themselves a palace in Florence. They, too, were once without a Porsche, so they bought themselves a Ferrari. So if you're one of those worn-out folks who aren't worth shit, then have mercy and take a hike, because they're calling security. They don't know from Mercy, there's no plastic surgeon in town by that name.

That's how things are on Bohemian, no way around it; the only thing democratic here is the blessed, distant din of the city and that stink that you can ultimately learn to love, a mix of garbage, fresh-baked muffins, the most expensive perfume, human caca, and scrap metal from the guts of the subway. The obsessive life of this district never lets up, illuminated through the night by the petrochemical glow of nearby brokerage houses.

It is here that Joanne Jordan worked, between Chase and the store that sold Ayurvedic cosmetics.

The salon itself was familiar to a lot of people because of its fairly clever name: *Hairdonism* . . . Oh boy . . . The owner, whose name is Jed, came up with it; he's big on art and likes to get in good with artists, or rather he has an unplacated, ever-intense grudge against karma for his not having been born one of them. And for a couple of other things as well.

Like many, he endeavors to kill this resentment that won't leave him alone with the aid of ethyl alcohol; in this he is consistent, patient, and impervious to his constant failures. Thus this grudge never seems to die, but on the contrary, as happens, basted in liters of wine, in undiluted whiskey and Stoli, it swells and sprouts one new thread after another, like buds, like nobody's business, it finds new objects and sweeps over each successive plane of his rather lonely mode of life.

Jed is a large, fat dude with a nice enough face that tends to flush all shades of red, by which one can judge accurately enough the degree of his unreality, from the slightest blush to the scarlet of an undercooked steak, replete with melancholic flecks. In decent jackets and Italian shoes, he tries to lend his place of business an artistic chic, stuffing every nook with incredibly random books bought in bulk (*Moby Dick, How to Love Your Osteoporosis, The Life and Death of Stalin, Weekend Decoupage, How to Be Like Elton John*). He claims that he had once wanted to study comparative literature, but then it seems he fell into drug addiction, which he's fortunately completely come out of, which doesn't happen that often . . . While he was going over all this, totally drunk, hand on his heart, it was impossible not to believe that he would make quite a good essayist. When she doesn't happen to have a client, Joanne sometimes looks into that odd book collection, reading random sentences aloud, using them to tell her fortune or else, in a pretty nonsensical manner, relating them to her own views on a given conundrum, such as:

"'Look, Candy,'" she read. "'This ol' dog jus' suffers hisself all the time.'" To which she immediately added, putting Steinbeck back on the shelf: "Poor dog. I hate when animals suffer."

Or else as she was now reading: "'Fortunately, I have what's left of my career and wonderful children.' Whoa, is that a sign? I've missed my period!"

"Again?" Mallery sighed, just on her way to get decolorant from the back.

"Again," Joanne says, sticking her tongue out at her, and picks up another book: "'For regions do not suddenly end, as far as I know, but gradually merge into one another.'"

That was too much for her.

"Nonsense," she said, turning up the radio (they were playing Beyoncé, whom she adored). "Beckett. Isn't he some kind of tennis player? One thing's for sure: dude's pretty batshit."

It was just as she was saying this that some girl walked into the salon.

Jed had just left for lunch (which usually consisted of gulping down ten glasses of wine at a nearby bar) (not the glasses, of course) (they were too non-alcoholic!) and, what with the receptionist's absence, it was Jo standing behind the counter. "Hi," the client said. "I'd like to get a trim."

"Mrs . . . ?"

"Loraz."

Jo caught a strong whiff of whiskey and was now trying, running her pen over the appointment book, to locate a name even a tad bit similar.

"Loraz, like the chain of grocery stores," the girl offered.

"Oh, Loraz, that's where I always do my shopping!" Joanne smiled. "Unfortunately, I don't have anyone by that name on the list," she added right away, confounded.

But the girl had already gone for a stroll along the bookshelves, as though she were of the opinion that you should never waste an opportunity to show the world your nonchalance. She had a stud in her nose, fur on her collar despite the warm weather, shoes from the twenties, and rainbow-striped socks. It was obvious she belonged to those messed-up kids from St. Patrick's, a postindustrial neighborhood on the river that's all the rage lately: that's precisely how they all look down there, like characters escaped from the pages of Philip K. Dick novels and trying to fit in among the earthlings while hiding from the interstellar police.

The girl touched each book in turn with the tip of her finger, like children who've suddenly gotten it into their heads that if they don't do it their mom is going to die.

"Chris loves this one," she said, pulling out *One Hand Clapping.* "He can read it all the livelong day."

"Did you have an appointment?"

"Honestly, I just popped in," the girl said, fiddling with a paper bag, in which she had a bottle. It was only then that Joanne noticed that she had mascara smeared across her face, as though she'd just stopped crying and had given herself a quick once-over with her shirt cuffs. "All I'd like is for someone to give me a haircut. It's not really such a big deal. I have to do it now."

"I'm sorry, our next opening isn't until . . ."

"Pretty please."

"I might be able to squeeze you in . . ."

"If you don't cut my hair, I'm walking right out of here, smashing a bottle, and trimming it myself."

•

Joanne froze over the appointment book. The girl was trembling all over. For some unknown reason, Jo had a sense that the girl wasn't kidding around. Without a word, she pointed her to a washbasin. *All my life with nutcases,* she thought.

"Can I smoke here?"

"Sadly, no."

"I ran out of the house and hopped on the subway. On the way I was howling the whole time, utter silence throughout the car, just my howl, I'm telling you. This is just where I got out, I don't even know where I am. I saw you through the window, and I thought: I need to cleanse myself, I have to rid myself of this, I need to tear it off me. That faggot'll see me and will know what he's done to me. He'll know what he's brought me to. He'll think I have cancer. That's what I want him to think! Or else that I'm locked up in a maximum-security prison. Because I've murdered him. *What a fag.* Shave it right down to the skin, please."

"Who was that?" Jed asked, passing her in the doorway and looking her over with satisfaction as she walked away: just as he'd dreamt, the artists were starting to get the wheel of industry turning, and just let somebody tell him it's not because of that book collection!

"I have no idea," Jo sighed, brushing aside her dark, clumpy, none-too-clean hair.

But that's how things were on Bohemian, and that's why people loved that street.

"How's it going with *your* baldy?" Jed asked. He spread out, lounging behind the counter where the receptionist

49

usually sat. He had bought himself a jar of cocktail onions and was nibbling them with whiskey. He was putting on the tone of a generous and understanding uncle, and from behind that smokescreen you could sense deep suffering. He was still *insufficiently* drop-down drunk *not* to suffer.

"Thanks. We want to take a vacation. If I can get time off, of course," Jo winked at him.

"Our playboy's still selling faucets, eh?"

"Fixtures," Jo reminded him, scratching at her chest.

"He doesn't fuck around on you? You know how women are affected by the sight of a guy who knows his way around plumbing."

"That's just his sideline. Soon there's supposed to be an opening at the Hungarian Cultural Institute."

"Then what? You'll embark on a great big journey to celebrate?"

"Exactly."

"You'll ride around Hungary on a great big sausage ring?"

"You guessed it, Jed. And we'll check out the ocean on the way; all my butt dreams of is being immersed in the ocean."

"Asshat," she thought. Something was eating him today. Despite being the owner and founder of Hairdonism, he was usually a pretty decent guy. Even if sometimes when he was drunk he tousled her hair too long or held her hand to his mouth, leaving tender kisses, much too intimate and wet for an employer. Once he even tried to suck on her fingertips; Jo indulged him these minor abominations, and afterward she would just discreetly wipe his spit off her hands and cheeks with a paper towel. Don't ask why: he was unhappy, and every so often a little tenderness should come his way, even if it's only his own tenderness and he doesn't even remember it afterward anyway. Joanne believed that even when his brain was drifting on its side like a leaky ship, awash in cheap whiskey, his soul, or else the *something* that a person has within, remembers those itty-bitty minutes of happiness and the soothing nearness of another person. Nothing remained of them, even the recollection of those caresses would be evacuated from Jed with the last drop of dark hangover urine, and yet even then a kind of warmth and mutual understanding arose between these two. It seemed that Jed regarded Jo as a kind of representative of the feminine component in his life, especially since she'd started coming in with her neckline covered in petechial effusions and smelling of lipstick, while her bra strap poked out from under her sleeve. And if you want to put it less philosophically: he liked her is all, and the pipe dreams he had of sleeping with her someday were taking over his sex life.

"Hold on, hold on, Jo, wait a second. I was showing you that session where I was styling models for a catalogue . . . now where was that?"

He broke off, seeing that Jo is rummaging through her handbag and pulling the pins out of her bun, leaving her hair to tumble down and spill over her shoulders like a tower knocked down by an airplane. He still wanted to keep her somehow, to win her over. In the salon there were only two clients, who were sitting there with their heads wrapped in foil, flipping through the cheaply printed atlases of stars' stubbly armpits, exploding breast implants, and deteriorating plastic surgeries, as well as of the various other entropic abominations that people can never get enough of. Warm sunlight fell against the front window, dappling the floor. Jed was rummaging frantically through the folders on his laptop, searching for some kind of evidence that he was worth sleeping with, or that it was at least worth considering. The icons on his desktop, however, were proliferating weirdly, doubling and slipping out from under his mouse's arrow.

"Honey, you've shown me that already," Jo tossed out blithely. She knew he was already drunk enough that she could allow herself a certain degree of blitheness toward him, impertinence even. "This is, like, the three hundred and twenty-first time."

"The one we had cutting hair back then . . . what was his name . . . ?" Jed kept stammering pitifully, like a schoolkid in a nightmare, with no hope of remembering the lesson he'd known perfectly just a moment before. Burping, he directed his embittered eyes toward her legs, too slim relative to the rest of her body, to the place where the seam drawn in felt-tip pen slid up beneath her leather skirt, which Jo complemented today with a frothy, creamy-laced blouse that smelled of vintage store and its original sweat from the seventies.

Joanne examined her roots in the mirror. She reached for one of the vials of coloring and slipped it into her sunflower-shaped handbag.

"You're leaving early again."

"I have to buy a swimsuit. I'm taking this. Be a dear and put it on my tab," she said, leaving him without a shadow of hope he'd see anything out of it. "Shade 014, artificial chestnut."

·

She left her application for vacation time on the countertop and sent Jed an absentminded kiss on her way out. Unfortunately, he was too drunk to catch it in midair, and the kiss flew out the window and attached itself to the cheek of some Chinaman driving past in a homemade shit heap, skewers loaded top to bottom with little paradise apples protruding from the trunk.

CHAPTER 7

A stinking big-city summer.

It was so sunny, so raucous and loud.

From among the leaves she was being observed by the cunning gaze of gray, hyperactive, excessively propagated squirrels, which scurry down from everywhere at the crackling of bags of pecans and bombard their benefactor with their worrisome eyes, importunate little noses, their flighty, yet insolent, presence.

The fault for this lay with various childless marriages, lovers making a show of their sensitivity for each other, children feeding the arrogant creatures the leftovers from their school lunch sandwiches, and tourists who've run out of things to do with the memory in their digital cameras. So if in the near future you plan to take part in the elimination rounds of the game show *Movies That Don't Exist Yet,* and you get a question about the horror *Deadly Squirrels 7D,* coming in two years to a theater near you and based on a true story, you'll know that it's all about the little square off Bohemian and the aren't-they-adorable little gray beasties now frolicking before Joanne's eyes among the leaves, tripping over their own fluffy, gracefully curved tails.

•

This profusion assaulting the senses brought Jo a kind of metaphysical titillation, a beguilement, some hankering that suddenly paralyzed her on all levels and that she was unable to put a name to. She thought only that she loved this city, that she loved life. This contained the characteristic modicum of pain at there not being more of her, that there weren't two of her. But that could just be hunger. For something suddenly seized her, and somehow, somewhere, she parked her Pinto, which resembled a trampled tin toad. The smell of lamb shawarma drove her so crazy that she took one right from a street vender and snarfed it down while standing with her legs somewhat apart, and her onion rings fell out and rolled under the legs of passers-by and farther down the street.

She was a Buddhist and a vegetarian, but in spite of this she was at times somehow unable to resist; she'd keep to her diet for a few weeks, and then some demon would drag her to one of the Yugoslav stores on St. Patrick's, where monumental rings of kielbasa writhed behind deli glass entwined with plastic ivy and fake lemons. Most often she ate a piece on the street, straight from the paper, munching on it with those weird rotten pickles of theirs.

Now, hounded by winos' taunts, she got into her Pinto. She let the wind pull the ticket for her poor parking from the wipers, popped a Mento into her mouth, and started inching her way through the traffic toward Bath. Just imagine her surprise when, wandering down the mall's main corridor . . .

"Farah, is it you?!" she shouted incredulously as she approached. "I wouldn't have recognized you at all!"

"Thanks," Farah blurted. "I'm going through a sort of transformation . . ."

"Oh no, don't change a thing: you look totally the same! These contacts are old; I haven't had time to buy new ones."

CHAPTER 8

As far as her neighbors were concerned, whose forks, remote controls, and MultiFitnessHomeTrainer oars were knocked out of their hands by her cries of ecstasy, and who at any rate had registered appropriate complaints with the building administration, well, Joanne never paid them much mind. She had keys made for her Hungarianist, he drove straight over from Tip-Tap Kitchen & Bath (you know the song they torture you with on the radio? Sometimes it follows me for days at a time, so much I can't get rid of it; I have just one thought looping around in my head, "For Tip-Tap faucets, get your faucets at Tip-Tap"). When he was still on his way in he unbuttoned and dropped his ill-conceived, sort of women's jeans; they made love as soon as she returned from work; anyway, it was all over a moment later, and all that remained of their love were a few fingernail scratches on the wood paneling, some hovering dust bunnies, some pubic hairs running amok on the parquet floor.

When she had rented this studio, there were even antlers hung up over here, and there was a scrap of real fur lying next to the bed; in spite of everything, someone was evidently trying to realize his dream of having a hunter's cottage in this pretty run-down house by the river. Whereas this sort of collecting, whose victims say "Oh how darling!" at the sight of just about anything that can be detached, removed, and brought home, made Joanne suffer. Two years into her sojourn here most of the paneling was covered by little pictures, postcards, photos, fliers for yoga schools, museum opening hours, brochures inviting you to join their sect, free sugars from cafes, and a Desideratum printed off the internet. In the middle of the room there was a shoddy red plastic table from Wal-Mart that she thought looked totally "designer," and she adored asking people how much she'd bought it for. "Go on, guess how much I could pay for that. Go on!" and everyone, to please her, said: fifty dollars. Which, in actual fact, was close: forty-two, and yet it looked like it could cost several hundred! ("Especially when someone takes out his contacts," Farah should have said, but it had occurred to her only later when she was already home.)

Stacked upon this table were the accoutrements of her not-too-well-thought-out, if passion-filled, life: a plastic Buddha light, intimate gel, ointment for the pimples that kept popping out over her neckline, Daim Bar wrappers, DVDs, eyeliner, packets of Tums. There was also a "personal massager" with a little Vader head, newsletters from the Jehovah's Witnesses that she'd pulled from her mailbox, a BBQueen Grill menu, her camera, high-heeled shoes with the leather scraped off that she never had the time or wherewithal to take in for repair and whose heels she was trying to bring to working order herself, with nail polish.

Who knows, maybe all these caresses, tender and fevered, the physical pleasure into whose waves they so eagerly dove, now daily, had brought these two to the verge of transcendence. Against which worldly things always appear as shabby, low-budget scenery, leaving the impression of children's toys. It would seem that this is why they were capable of not taking in the nastiness of this tiny apartment: it seemed not to concern them, to be meaningless in the context of their erotic passion. Now, too, they couldn't have it any better but to lie on the not-quite-vacuumed rug, where rainbow-colored triangles were supposed to represent the infinitude of the cosmos. Empty, unrefined, unaware of how bad they look naked, they allowed the warm, botanical-smelling air from over the river to drape their love-battered, red-splotched bodies in soothing kisses. From Water Street, where the windows opened, there fell the impatient calls of little lead-caked birds, the sounds of soaring aeroplanes, and the roar of the el rolling across the overpass.

"I can't," Jo sighed, picking a ball of dust and hair out of the rug, raising it to her eye, and putting it back down. "I can't get used to the thought that one day…"

"What, Jo?"

"That I'm going to die."

"That what?!"

"That I'm going to kick it. Everyone will go on living their lives, and I'll be lying like a cat in the street, with cars just speeding by."

"Don't talk like that."

"Well it's true," Jo said, and a mascara-blackened tear tumbled down her cheek.

"Just think how many people have died already."

"What about it?"

"Nothing. Life goes on!"

"That's supposed to make me feel better?!" Jo said, her voice cracking. "I don't want to. I love life too much. I know that I'm a Buddhist, and even though from that perspective I shouldn't think this way . . ."

"But . . . ?"

"Every time we're done making love, I'm seized by something so sad. As if I had an emptiness inside, and if someone were to hit me it could only produce a dull boom. As if the wind were blowing right through me! When you take me, I feel so full, so strong, alive, and when it's over this intense loneliness envelops me again. I know that we're two foreign bodies once again, that a connection is impossible, that a person is alone within herself forever . . ."

"Jo!" the Hungarianist said placatingly, attempting to plug her mouth with a kiss.

"Friendship or love, it only makes everything worse, it gives you illusions. You think you're close to somebody, then you happen to run into him at the store, you tell him, 'I'm driving to the ocean,' and he's not happy for you at all. He's not happy for your happiness! You're in love with somebody, and now you're thinking that he'll be another you with you, that you'll be stuck together and it'll always be that way, head to head, heart to heart, that you'll burn that loneliness away, all the fat of life, the crushing abomination of your very existence, burn it all on the great bonfire of your love! And meanwhile: all he does is get up and go to the bathroom to take a piss, and you're lying there looking at the mounds of cellulite that had once been your thighs!"

"Don't cry, Jo, I'm begging you," he said, kissing away her tears. "It's all going to be fine."

"Stop trying to calm me down and shut me up!" Jo exclaimed. "I see no reason to be calm, since clearly I'm not! I don't want to be calm when I'm not calm! It's my right!"

"All I was saying was . . ."

"I know what you're trying to say, and I'm imploring you: don't!"

"But . . ."

"*No, this isn't PMS!*" she screamed.

But it was too nice out to sulk for long, and a moment later they were once again sunk in kisses and moans. The sun went down, washing the sky in thick pink, and they opened a bottle of sour chardonnay. A lot of crumbled cork fell inside, but they managed to get their money's worth of drunk. He, watching *CSI*, scratched at his balls, and with his fingers he combed a few hairs to make them grow a little, as though he wanted to extract all possible use from them before they fell out: wind it around a finger and let it blow in the wind, twist it into braids and tug at it while yawning . . . Whereas Joanne was walking through the house in a worn T-shirt, dye on her roots, taking care of various things. She was examining articles of clothing for stains, trying to scratch some of them off with her fingernail; she attempted to scrub the seams from her legs, but they didn't want to come off, not with rubbing alcohol, nor with shampoo; she spoke on the phone with her brother . . .

(As far as his story goes, Dean Jordan was living in San Diego and dealing old computer games, mailing them to enthusiasts the world over, from which he could just barely make ends meet. And though his mess of an apartment, where he was crammed together with his wife and young son, was packed floor to ceiling with boxes of *Prophecy*, *Bat*, and *Koshan Conspiracy*, still shrink-wrapped since 1993 with the sheets of cardboard and the air that secured the packages, gave off a pretty ridiculous impression, and was an object of scorn for the entire family, Jo thought his job was totally cool and "full of imagination." Or at least that's what she said every time his spirits were down.)

("Dean," she was now saying, "you can't stop believing in what you're doing! You yourself were saying that this month you were selling some guy shitloads of games . . . People like him need you, goddammit! Besides, just imagine, you pack up these games, take them to the post office, and . . . Right now they might already be somewhere totally far away, somewhere like Poland, or the Former Yugoslavia! The world is so huge! There are so many continents and different countries that we have no clue. It's awesome, Dean, I envy you!")

She was shifting objects from one place to another and analyzing ads from oceanside motels so as to minimize the likelihood of athlete's foot—when she ran into her today at the mall, Farah had tried to convince her that motels, their carpeting as well as their wading pools, are full of these spores or thalli or some such.

Finally: she was executing sloppy asanas and talking to herself. Perhaps you, too, are in the habit of seeing this as irritating, but in my opinion it contained a kind of deep self-acceptance and sympathy for one's own person.

"Oh, Christ!" she would say, for example, unexpectedly, not anticipating, or rather not wishing for herself, that somebody might ask, "What happened?" "My gold card at Meditation Studio's about to run out! I'll lose my discount."

Or:

"Chloe. Chloe may well be the prettiest name for a girl. I like Mae, too, but Chloe is the prettiest."

Or:

"Hey, maybe it *was* PMS! I just got my period!"

She was slightly disappointed: she had secretly believed she might be pregnant. It was a little exciting: being *maybe* pregnant. She imagined herself this way practically every month: paunches are soooooo sexy! But maybe it really was better this way: the world wasn't headed in a good direction, who knows how long it would all last. Ten years? Twenty? What right did she have to bring another individual into a place of such uncertain awesomeness and to condemn her to suffering and pain? Well, and there was something still much worse: she didn't like his last name. For real! She'd already tried it on. Chloe Tyrd? Mae Tyrd, that was a little better, but not by a lot. And besides: when was she actually supposed to have this child? Work at Hairdonism, sex, meditation, yoga, she had practically no time for herself. She didn't even have time to buy herself new contact lenses so that she could see what she was actually doing!

"Damn, I have heartburn again," she said. She had just found a ring of rindy chorizo on the table and was looking at it, lost in thought. "Can you imagine, today I ran into Farah."

"Farah? How's she doing? Seems she hasn't been hanging around with us much lately . . ."

"Oh, stop it."

"Didn't she have fun with us that time at the IMAX?"

"Oh God, don't remind me," Joanne said with a laugh, rolling her eyes at the memory of that evening that was hard to forget; they'd gotten so drunk, and it was terrible the way they had, right next to her . . . Needless to say, it was downright boorish! Hee hee.

"Maybe she's run out of antibacterial gel and can't leave the house."

"She's alone. That's why she acts that way."

"Don't defend her. Anyway, you know . . ."

"Sometimes it seems the chick's losing it, she needs to find someone," Joanne said, and she glanced vigilantly toward the door. A shiver passed through her: for a moment it seemed that Farah was standing in the doorway and listening to all of this.

"If you ask me, she's a dyke."

"She is not!"

"Is."

"It's only because of those shoes she wears."

"Something along the lines of 'hiking heels'? They make her look like she's constantly going down to the cellar to get jam for her tea."

Hold on, let me go get my quince! Last summer I pickled two thousand jars of it. Nobody eats it, it's getting all moldy! I do hope this gives you an appropriate sense of guilt.

"But what gets me is that she never goes out with us anymore," Joanne said. It really did make her sad. Honestly, it wasn't the same without Farah, something was always missing, her envy would make everything more attractive and exciting. Jo's qualms got the better of her. "It's just that she doesn't know how to make herself up," she added in her friend's defense. "After all, she could be quite pretty!"

"Don't make me laugh."

"Fine, then: slim. And besides that, she has lovely hair."

"True that. *She has hair.* That's an asset for sure. But enough with the praise already. You want to order some dinner?"

CHAPTER 9

September 29.

Dear Diary.

*The chickens from BBQueen Grill that wanted to avenge my hav-
ing scarfed down their wings late last evening should probably be
quite satisfied. UTTER VENGEANCE ACCOMPLISHED!
After scarfing them down I gained ten pounds, and now I might
not be able to squeeze into the bathing suit I just bought in downtown Bath. Dead Head Jed gave me time off, and we're getting out
of here any minute—that is, of course, if this scrap heap doesn't
fly into pieces under me on the first beltway. Last evening it was
already repeating on me tremendously, I had total heartburn, and
then I dreamed such stuff as to make Oedipus's Odyssey look
like a subway ride two stops and back. Oh, Jordan, why must
you always be such a disgusting "maybe-just-a-tiny-bit-more" and
"just-this-piece-of-skin"?*

*Anyway, maybe there are other reasons: I took an Advil because
my period hurt, and beyond that I ran into Fah at the store and
came away with the impression that between us there's some jeal-
ousy on her part. I have no idea what it could be about, but things
are not the same between us as they once were, I felt bad vibes,
maybe she figured out what we were up to that time next to her
at the IMAX ;)) , but that's a little no fair! At any rate, I dreamed*

*we were at the beach lying on beach chairs, and the cool salt breeze
was blowing over our sweaty bodies. It was D-lite-full, sipping on
the best Campari and juice and reading this totally interesting article in* Yogalife . . .

The controversial article Joanne was reading just happened to concern the inherent loneliness of human life on
Earth. The author, a professor at Bengson University, con-
cluded that love does not exist, while what we are in the
habit of taking for love is merely the absurd hope that
another individual is in a position to free us from ourselves,
to incorporate us, absorb us, liberate us from the oppressive
obligation of being us.

I completely agree! thought Joanne, taking a deep swig of
her Campari.

"Of course, nothing of the kind has any right to happen," the article announced. "We are alone till the end,
nothing will help us, not alcohol, nor drugs, nor the quizzes
they have there on Facebook, nor our genitals. Yes, even the
last of these, sort of slightly resembling monsters, created as if
specifically for lovemaking, for transcendent acts of joining
two into one, are good for anything *but*. Who makes love in
order to be unified, to join with another, to merge into spiritual and physical unity?"

"That's right," Joanne whispered, pimples on her face,
utterly unaware that the water level in the ocean was getting
weirdly lower. The text affirmed certain observations and
anxieties of hers that she had been incapable of expressing.
In its subsequent passages, it offered postulates for stripping

love of the "transcendence complex" and "metaphysical pipe dreams" and dealing with it with illusion-free creativity.

When Joanne tore herself momentarily away from this passionate reading, she was struck dumb with terror. It had turned out that in the meantime someone had been pumping all the water out of the ocean. All that was left was wet sand, upon which lay suffocating fish and withering jellyfish, chunks of surfboards and passenger ships, dead crabs and old washing machines.

Dear Diary, I was so sorry for all those creatures and for the ice cream tossed out when children had hardly touched it, but most of all for myself, since I thought that it'll surely be another hundred years before I get time off again, and by that time I might be able to fit one thigh into my Sponge B. swimsuit. In this dream I was thinking that it must have been Jed who'd let the damn water out, he's massively jealous that I have someone, you can even see it in my subconscious.

The moral of all this is, first of all: no more heavy food at night. When I get home from vacation, a diet of only vegetables and 0% yogurt :)) FUCK IT ALL.

CHAPTER 10

Obviously: what would have been best that time they ran into each other at the mall is if she'd squealed: "Oh, it's wonderful you're going," "Of course it'll be fantastic, Jo," "I'm so happy for you," and so forth. That would have been best, we get it. But on the other hand, for whose sake was she supposed to have done that when she was trembling all over with anger, with a resentment toward Joanne that had suddenly returned in all its abundance, as though it hadn't disappeared at all during these last weeks but had merely drifted off to the side somewhere in order to proliferate and gather its strength?

"I once went to the ocean, too," she said. "With my mom and my brother."

"Really?" Jo asked while paying significantly more attention to fondling some bra.

"It was before my dad died; I was five. All I remember is my delight left me speechless, and that I cried when I was dragged away."

"It must have been sad for you," Joanne said dispassionately while snapping a clasp.

"You have to be careful at the motel. There's usually a ton of athlete's foot in the carpeting and showers."

"What are you talking about? Where are we going to make love? Joking."

"And it's always better to check whether they've over-charged your credit card. I'm not kidding. It happens quite often. Oh, and don't look under the bedsheet—that's obvious. I did once, and I'm warning you, I couldn't eat anything afterwards."

"For all these twenty-four years?"

"Sorry?"

"Well . . . You said you were there when you were five . . . Never mind. It was a joke."

("Maybe you should warn people when you're joking?" Farah could have told her. "Then they'd know when to laugh." But in the end all she said was:)

"Boy . . . I envy you. At the agency today it was all I could do not to faint from the heat."

"Maybe you should take off somewhere?"

"Maybe."

"Fah, you work too much! Some rest would do you good."

"Maybe I'll go to the pool."

"I can't stand the pool," Jo said. "I can't stand those caps, they make people look like peanuts."

"I have to lose a few pounds. I've gained some weight lately." Here Farah cast a casual but meaningful eye at the Sephora display, in which, next to the reflection of a stocky Jo in her frothy blouse, her own figure, thin and supple, was wavering. From a distance they must have looked like a flamingo chatting with an obese hedgehog before a match at the Queen's. "I'm disgustingly fat."

Obviously, Jo pretended not to hear. She suddenly started to look for something most urgently in her handbag.

"Fine, then, since you're not going to take yourself

anywhere," she said, "maybe you'd like a ticket to an opening? I got them yesterday from some wacked-out artist. She
showed up without an appointment and demanded that we
cut her hair, and when I did all of a sudden she said, 'Oh
yeah, so this is going to be volunteer work, I have minus two
dollars on my card.' Can you imagine? This town is full of
hopeless wackos. She ended up giving me these tickets. It's
apparently an awesome show. If not for my trip . . . I adore
contemporary art. It's so atypical."

"Thanks, but . . ." Farah said sourly. She was eyeing the
scrap of paper, entitled *Trash Hospital*. "This isn't a ticket."

"It's not?"

"She just gave you some flier for cutting her hair, Jo.
And a very poorly designed one at that."

"It's a bit far, but you could get there."

"It's in Princetown, Jo."

"There's a bus that goes."

("Maybe I'll go catch it right away, so that come Friday
I'll already be there," Fah should have answered at the time.
But, of course, it only occurred to her significantly later.)

"Thanks, I appreciate the 'gift.' But I'm not traveling
an hour to look at a Starbucks cup held together with a
Band-Aid."

"You could meet someone . . ."

It's a wonder how some can cram so much into a single,
apparently smallish gaze!

By which Fah now informed Joanne what she thinks on
the topic of hospitals for trash and their pinko founders. Who
should be admitted there themselves and get treatment for
their teeth, never before touched by an orthodontist; their
dreadlocks, swimming in suet; their rat-infested apartments;

and their pretentious ideas about life. To your health! Let them smoke marijuana, French kiss their hellos, and eat their food with the same hands that a moment earlier held measles and rotavirus.

"Oh well, I have to run, it's terribly stuffy here. And besides, I have to pack."
"I have to run, too!"
("I have a meeting at Joannaholics Anonymous," she could have said then. "Today my coach and I are going to work on getting me to stop sniffing the sweater you once left at my place.")

She returned home and dug out her swim cap.
She tried it on in the mirror, and tears were rolling down her cheeks. A moment later she was already howling her head off. She was trembling all over, not knowing what was up with her. No, she didn't at all look like a peanut, she looked like a fetus suffering from hysteria! Joanne just had to spoil everything for her, trample her slightest joy. Poison her, rob her of her happiness! Destroy her transformation. Yes, she had destroyed her transformation! "You haven't changed a bit, it's these contacts!" What, so to her it was nothing? All her work on herself, all her efforts, purchases, the careful nutrition was now burning up wholesale on the pile of a single "you haven't changed a bit." She couldn't not look at her roots, the makeup crookedly applied, the careless depilation of the upper lip, the Sponge Bob bathing suit that Jo had waved before her very nose! She felt she could explode any minute, that she'd start screaming, banging her head against the wall, tearing down the curtains.

Finally, without so much as taking off the bathing cap, she took a razor from the medicine cabinet and carefully disinfected it. She thought for a moment about the right place, and then she started dragging it along the back of her leg, down her thigh and further down her calf, so that it looked like a seam. The skin put up resistance and made a scraping sound, which made her feel nauseous, and she whimpered with pain and regret, and in the end . . . in the end she cut herself! But that had been the whole point. To cut herself—in the end, it was *her* she, *her* I, she could do with it as she pleased, she could chop off her own head and put it in on the dresser, "Guess how much I paid for it," she'd ask everyone, if she got a hankering to do so. "Go on, guess. I got it for free! It was sitting on me when I was born!"

No one would stop her! No one was going to tell her what she had to do, no longer would anyone drag her hither and thither by the nose! Slash yourself—nay, slash your mother . . . your grandmother . . . slash Joanne and the whole world. She surrenders her life to grievance! It'll be a *relief* . . . relief . . . a banal, easy-to-locate physical pain will bring about a violent liberation from the internal, limitless one flowing from her heart and will drown every cell of her reason; the incisions will bleed and hiss when she washes them in water and peroxide and . . . and . . .

She would have done it for sure, yes, she was ready, she could already picture it, but it was her misfortune that something had tempted her into looking at the mirror. She saw her own face, red, covered in flecks of snot, in her bathing cap, and in a fraction of a second the absurdity of this vision overpowered her. Her skin turned out to be thick and stubborn, and she succeeded in excavating no more than two smallish notches. She wrapped the razor in toilet paper and hid it at the very bottom of the garbage bag.

CHAPTER II

The air smelled of salt. She crossed the beach and entered the water, cold, green, salty, endless.

She dove in and swam, but the fact that she had been underwater for a long time, without access to air, made no difference to her, so much so that she was surprised how easy it was: she breathed quite normally, despite descending deeper and deeper. *Was all that equipment some kind of scam?!* she thought as she passed coral reefs brimming with schools of rainbow-colored fish, which swam past old French fries and shopping bags. *Turns out there's plenty of oxygen in the water.*

The deeper she went, the darker it got, and before she knew it she found herself on the bottom of the ocean. *It has to be here somewhere,* she thought confidently, looking at the old washing machines and bits of surfboard and hulls of sunken ships, the Jack Daniels bottles, among which haggard, contaminated mermaids were poking around like homeless people.

"Are you looking for someone?" one of them asked as it swam up to her. She had a hoarse voice, a California accent, and the shifty eyes of a train-station swindler. She must have been pretty once; she had dark eyes and pockmarked skin; her hair was tied back with a K-Mart bag. "I can help you."

"I'm looking for the ocean's drain," Fah said.

"Its what?"

"Its drain. Do you know where it is?"

"Its discharge?" the other repeated uncertainly, and Farah noticed her tail, diseased, the scales flaking off, patched with Band-Aids, beneath which you could see the inflamed, diseased skin. "Sure. It's really close."

"Where?"

"For a liter of vodka, I'll tell you."

"I don't have any vodka."

What was she to do? Just now, before her eyes, a soggy, visibly wave-swept issue of *Yogalife* floated by. She grabbed it and, separating clumped-together pages, read a rather illegible, yet shocking, article about the following unsettling circumstance . . .

". . . due to which the mermaids are threatened with extinction. Overcome by a fascination with humans and their human world, dozens of these creatures swim our entire waterfront every year, taking everything people throw away back down to their lairs, constructing bizarre camps on the bottom of the ocean supposedly in imitation of the human world. They build these out of, among other things, the black boxes of disintegrated airplanes, Coke cans, old boots, barbed wire, and scraps of wetsuit. They put on bikini tops that have been swept away by waves, try to fit the ends of their tails into unpaired flip-flops and ocean-tossed sunglasses. For many years now the marine police have kept mum about seduction and abduction of the more daring of our sunbathers, and especially of divers, so that they can then spend entire days gazing lovingly upon their faces, already washed featureless by the waters, stroking them and covering them with kisses. An equally tragic phenomenon is how they have become addicted to the heroin left in needles that people have thrown into rivers, as well as to sucking on bottles for their last drops of high-proof alcohol, which has a particularly powerful and addictive effect on their organism. Consequently, 50 percent of them . . ."

"Nice pants," the mermaid said, feeling the pajama fabric. "Give them to me, and I'll show you where the drain is."

With childish delight she pulled the legs of Farah's pajamas over her arms and slipped into the dark turquoise depths. Despite her dilapidation and the fact that her tail flapped in only one direction, she swam lightyears faster and more efficiently than Fah, who was left behind now and again. She felt awful without the pants she had to give away—the ocean was constantly flowing into her and dribbling out her mouth, and little fish and Fanta bottlecaps were tickling her ovaries and lungs. She kept thinking that she could hear someone shouting "bare ass! bare ass!"—but she didn't know where these crude jeers could be coming from, and anyway, it was probably just alcohol-addled seahorses. She finally came to a stop, helpless, gasping, leaning on the hull of a busted motorboat. She waited. After a while the mermaid swam out from behind a great reef. She had wrapped the pants in a great big bow around her head. A tangle of old, broken Christmas lights trailed from her tail.

"I asked around a bit," the mermaid said. "Regarding your . . . I don't know what it is you're looking for. It's probably here somewhere."

As she said this, she waved a hand a little to the left, a little to the right.

"Where?" Farah asked helplessly, looking around at the mounds of garbage all around them.

"Here!" the mermaid snapped, now gesturing forward and back. "I don't have an infinite amount of time to show you, I said I'd show you where it was, not that I'd look for it with you."

"In that case give me back my pants."

"I can't."

"Why not?"

"They're tied tight. And besides, I promised them to my sister, she's going to be laying her eggs soon. Though she says they're all bloody, and nothing will come of them."

In what remained of her dream Farah was raking her hands through the sand, now and then chancing upon hairpins, rings, fake teeth, and curlers. Toward morning, she finally found a stopper on a rusty chain. She gave it a yank. The water instantly started to whirl, bubble, and go down, down, down from the ocean, faster and faster and faster . . .

And to think that this had all happened on account of poor Jed, who didn't know what he was dreaming about that night because he was too drunk for that. She woke up half naked; her pajama bottoms were lying in the foyer.

CHAPTER 12

And what had gotten into her head to make her *actually go* to that opening after all?

Perhaps that it was Friday. Friday! Beware, all you nondrinkers, nonsmokers, the sexually unattractive, the neurotic, the disturbed, those down in the dumps, those who don't have five million friends on Facebook. Old folks, those who breastfeed and for that reason can't get stoned, those who don't own a Lamborghini, fat chicks, those who don't look good in dresses consisting solely of shoulder strap and shorts made out of only belt. Hide: the untanned, the unglittered, those who don't know how to squeal, the pregnant, those who get around in wheelchairs, those with cellulite and excessive sweating, bulimics, those who want to raid the fridge in peace, workaholics, those who just have to write a supplemental report that no one needs for any reason, computer geeks, those who beat the fuck out of mutants with a pixelated club, and slobs and losers of any other stripe. Or else simply gobble down a pound of Bordax, shut the windows, close the curtains, and, having plugged your ungroomed ears, sleep a hard sleep without surrendering to the terror of Friday-night fun.

This drives me to depression. The city has already started shaking by about six, and then it roars well into the night, full of shouts, squeals, stupid laughter, snapping heels, bottles clinking, champagne corks shooting into the air, coke snorted off toilet lids, and condoms stretched onto members . . . A whole week of processing one's single, unrepeatable, inexorably passing life into money must end in hilarity, in a bestial cry that "I have a right to a modicum of freedom!!!" Even if that hectic freedom, realized wholesale, and which has to suffice for the whole week following, means a right to freely make oneself into a dumbass, to tear the mucus membranes of one's genitals to shreds, and then to sleep with one's head in the shitter.

"Aren't you coming with us tonight for karaoke? It could be fun!" Ingeborg yelled after her from the reception desk like she was being all innocent, though Farah could have sworn there was a sneer in her voice, the suggestion that Farah never goes *anywhere*.

"I don't think so. I have to . . ."

"Look after your little nephew?"

"No, like, why would I have to look after him?"

Farah stopped. In fact, she turned around! Why are they picking on her? What's this about her nephew? So that's how it is? Poor Farah, that social cripple, can only look after other people's brats? Even if she doesn't do that ever and says she does only so that she doesn't have to spend every Friday going to that stupid, embarrassing karaoke?

A band of desperados, Farah thought disdainfully, with a hatred she'd suddenly assumed. Every Friday they reserved a booth at a Japanese club, always under the name "Mr. Ass," which every Friday turned out to be precisely as funny as it had been, i.e., *very funny.* They'd been laughing themselves silly over that joke since morning already. They took two taxis there; they devoted the first half of the evening to conversation about who had written and read what on Facebook until they finally got hammered and howled themselves ragged as an old pair of panties until midnight, so that the room reeked unbearably afterward. Whatever, in the end there had to be enough hardy adventure for an entire week of lunchtime storytelling and choking with laughter. ("And then Jake says, 'Where's my glass?' *While holding it in his hand!!!*") ("And you remember how Joe got confused and went into the ladies' room??? For the life of him he couldn't understand what had happened, not until that funny Japanese potty suddenly squirted him in the face!!!") Of course, the more loudly and colorfully they told it, the more likely they were all in bed by 12:15, smeared head to toe in dry-heel cream.

"Friday—tedious, crazed fun in my circle of coworkers—four hours"—they could check it off on the calendar and proceed to further urgent duties.

Obviously, at that point Farah still had no intention of going to some idiotic opening. She'd said that only to shut that moronic Ingeborg's mouth. But hardly had she gotten through her door than the doorbell rang. She peered through the peephole. It was that neighbor she'd met in the laundry, the one with the psychotropics and the perfect states of mind.

It would have been a good idea simply not to open the door. But you would have had to have told her that before she hit on another idea that lay much nearer.

"Hello?" she said.

"It's the end of the world. They're evacuating the building."

That might have perhaps been the one thing that would somehow justify letting him in.

"Hi," he said instead, with that characteristic pluck.

"Hi," Farah responded.

"I thought you were still at work," he explained.

"So then what are you doing here?" she asked suspiciously.

"There's something I have to talk to you about. Can I come in?"

"Not really."

"Why not?"

"Because I was just leaving."

"What for? It's Friday."

"That's right. I'm going to an opening."

"It'll only take a minute. My doctor is suggesting that I might go out somewhere on Fridays. It would be part of my therapy. It would be a slow, controlled return to normal life. I could get off the pharmaceuticals gradually, very gently, smoothly, though I'll probably be taking them for the rest of my life. Of course I told him right away that it's quite impossible, that I don't even know anybody, I don't have a lot of acquaintances who are into the nightlife. But he told me just to have a look around, surely someone else out there is lonely besides me, in a similar situation to mine, maybe even worse, who doesn't have anywhere to go either and is just waiting to be invited, so . . ."

("Right," Fah could have answered him then. "What are we going to go see? *Bloody Stepdad 2*? *Eat My Brain with a Ladle, Just Don't Slurp*? *Honey, I Killed the Cats*?")

·

Of course, she just came up with that now, standing alone before that cockeyed gallery.

"Hey, look where you're standing!" some kid just shouted, and only now did she hear the characteristic rattle of a skateboard on asphalt, the approach of which her ears had indeed registered for some time, but as though they were someone else's ears. She awoke from her reverie just as she was jolted by the air mass he dragged behind him. The great pink tarp of evening was stretching across the sky; the echo of some concert and the throng's joyous squeals arrived from the distance. In her hand she was holding a small mug of sour wine that made her breath reek. Sky-blue threads of marijuana wisped across the air like gossamer.

The bus had taken over an hour to get here; with a wistful gaze, she skimmed the passing housing developments flecked with the illumination of the first kitchen lights, accident-deformed cars shaking with hip-hop cranked up full blast, and basketball courts built by the mayor in a wave of pre-election hysterics, and upon which the only things now playing were layers of leaves having a round of "we're starting to rot."

She mingled into a group of insane apostates. With their woolen beards, which their fingers were constantly kneading, they looked as if a herd of goats had been freshly processed, and now they were rejoicing together over their equally distributed spoils. One of them handed Farah a joint, but then, when she told him in all honesty that her name wasn't Tracy, he took it back, and F. was again standing on her own, observing the old ladies with their hearing aids.

Though it was difficult for them to hide the fact that of all the pieces on display they were most intrigued by the free snacks, so as not to leave the artist empty-handed they made a decent round of the exhibit immediately after consuming them, announcing a couple of sonorous opinions that wouldn't hurt anyone ("that's different," "and unusual!").

Striking a blow against the bourgeois attachment to convention and those small, hypocritical rituals, the exposition presented shreds of slashed bedsheet, among other things. They seemed to be screaming, "No, honey, no, if you think making art means taking thirty years to paint some fat lady and child with a background of arcades bathed in sunlight, you're way off the mark. Better to spend thirty seconds slashing a bedsheet to shreds and designate the rest of that time for smoking ganja, muttering under your breath, laughing at YouTube videos, and walking into traffic signs."

There was also a bicycle festooned with rubber grapes with the inscription "Guantanamo," as well as a kiddy potty with a little infant turd made from puffy bouclé yarn.

She had no idea who these people around her were. She couldn't seem to classify them. Honestly, they looked like they'd been smeared in glue and dunked in a bin of donated clothes. Then again, what fashionable person doesn't look like that nowadays? The only one who attempted to connect with Farah turned out to be a scruffy, rumpled dude with breasts.

"Did you like the exhibit?" he asked in a high voice, and the impressive shred of romaine lettuce hanging from the corner of his mouth testified to the fact that before striking up this discussion he had fortified himself, thereby also spicing the opinions he professed with an intense aroma of smoked salmon. The fact that she hadn't answered didn't put him off in the least. "She's extremely political, in my opinion. One can't stay silent any longer . . . Have you ever heard of lizard people?"

Huh?
Nothing will ever change now, she thought, utterly indifferent to the fact that radical reflections that use such big words are best left to the idiots. Let them go around saying them to themselves on rainy days, while every atom of reality that hears them is, out of pure contrariness, already breaking ranks, turning tail, and starting to head in the complete opposite direction.

"You happen to have any smokes?"

At first she thought it was some boy.
"You smoke?" he said, being a girl.
"Actually . . ." Fah said, staring at her hair, shaved hellishly down to the very skin.
"Are you here alone?" the other immediately asked, as though she wanted to say, "Oh, let's not bother our little heads with your stupid answers!" At the same time, she was constantly looking around like people do when they are waiting for someone but just haven't decided yet for whom, so they have to keep checking to see whether that person might happen to be somewhere nearby.
"Never mind. You smoke?"
She had a stud in her nose, jazzy rainbow-striped socks, and a men's shirt decked out with a ruddy threadbare collar. Her neck was a little dirty, but just go ahead and give

85

it a scratch, it would surely turn out that this was a point of style, it'll be all the rage in two seasons, something you Birkenstock dandies obviously know nothing about!

"Do you know Peter?" she asked a moment later, and having caught someone with cigarettes she placed one between her own lips and another between Farah's.

"No," Farah admitted.

"You don't know the guy who did all this? Peter, he's totally cult. He's curating our entire show! This is his gallery. I once slept in his stairwell . . . That is, in the hall. You want me to introduce you? Peter? Peter! This is . . . What's your name? This is a girl I just met. Never mind, he can't hear us. The two of you might hit it off."

"Really?" Farah asked, just to say anything, to her own amazement extinguishing her cigarette on her sole, which she once saw in some movie.

"And that's his girlfriend next to him, Dominique," the girl said, pointing at that guy with the breasts who was talking Farah's ear off earlier about the lizard people. "She plays great on the oboe."

"Far out," Fah said.

"Well then, it was nice to meet you. I need to make the rounds a bit, there are a lot of people with a capital 'P' here. Sucking up to the bigwigs, it's the artist's lot."

"Does that mean that your work . . . ?" Farah went on asking, because she really didn't want the girl to go away.

"You could say that," she answered.

"Which one?"

"Did you see the fliers?"

"Yes."

"I designed them. Oh, it's Jasper! Jasper?"

Farah followed her chaotic maneuverings with an uncertain gaze. Everything moved so quickly, the data came in rapid succession, not in linked pairs or even bundles. Jasper loped around them like the face of the "Soft Drugs Are Bad, Too" campaign.

"I've known him for over a year. Our jackets were hanging on the same hook in the coatroom at a The Fires concert."

"Really?" Farah asked, because that's the only thing that occurred to her.

"Yeah. I'm going to the ladies'. You can come with me if you want."

"Why not?"

A moment later and she was already pressing behind the girl through something that, only by dint of the smallish dimensions of the Lizard's Stomach gallery, one might call a crowd.

"I'll introduce you to everybody, cool?" the girl asked.

"Everybody" turned out for the most part to be the bearded man who'd earlier classified her as Tracy ("Damn, it's you!" he said, and his lips parted into a smile: his fifteen-minute mental cycles apparently allowed him to experience the same things over and over for the first time) and a couple of other goat-plunderers who didn't even tell her their names—maybe they were no longer entirely sure of them themselves. As compensation, they greeted her effusively, pressing her lips with sour, juicy kisses that smelled of old Druid. It might have seemed that they really missed her, not having known her these many years. "Farah," she mumbled, unaccustomed to such directness, and . . .

"*What's that?!*" Go screamed from behind the lavatory door, with a pearly stream of urine for a background.

"Farah," she said, swallowing her saliva embarrassedly. "But call me 'Fah.'"

"Damn. And in grade school did they call you Farah Fatset?"

"Yeah," Farah admitted, blushing. "Or Farfel. After that it was always how I felt. Like farfel stuffing."

"One might have predicted that. Well, not your mom, I guess. What do you do . . . *Farah?*"

"I work at—" Farah said.

"I work too. That is, I flit a bit here, a bit over there. Since Chris and I broke up, I can't sit still. That is, we live together, but I need to keep occupied. So now I got a job at Mr. Foods on St. Patrick's. Not a bad gig, a cheerful team. I myself don't know yet what area of art interests me most. I'm drawn to too many different things. Theoretically I could write, I could paint, I could do performance, I went to video school. But that's theoretically. I don't have patience for anything. Everything bores me within two minutes. I start drawing a picture, and a minute later I'm looking out the window, I'm listening to the sounds of the city as they happen, and already I'd have gone someplace, I'd have gone back to living, not sitting there drawing some stupid picture. I write short stories, and after one sentence I think to myself, Come on, I'm not going to sit here like an idiot describing something that never existed, there are so many more interesting things all around me: concerts, exhibits, insane benders, and these *exist* through and through, and I have nothing on them, you know? I'm a logical person, I need something concrete."

Con-crete—that's more or less how she broke it up.

"I'm too rational. Besides, when it comes right down to it"—she continued when they'd pressed through to the bar—"you know what puts me off creating? The fact that any rando out there can all of a sudden become an artist. He'll take this bunch of basil, shove it up his urinary tract, and make a big fuss about it being his messed-up childhood! That's why my art that I do is just the fliers I design. That's my imperative: they're fast to make, and you don't need to spend hours pondering which great universal thought about human life on Earth to talk people into, how it was in them the whole time! What are you drinking?"

"Biowater C," Farah said to the bartender.

"Are you nuts?! We'll take two doubles on the rocks."

They worked efficiently, quickly, aimlessly. "Hey, Tracy, you sweet thing," the bearded boy said, handing Farah a joint; the girl's almond-shaped eyes smiled at her through the smoke; they ordered another round of whiskeys and sipped them with beer that someone had given them to hold; Dominique was playing the oboe. She saw the girl take a cigarette from someone and stick it behind her ear. With each drink Farah was more surprised, more bewitched, that such a totally nutty . . . such a . . . a . . .

"Have I told you my name?" Go asked. "It'll totally weird you out. It's Go."

"Go?"

"Gosza. But try having a name like Gosza. No one can pronounce it, so it just became Go. So my name is Move," she sighed. "Though perhaps my name is really Get Moving.

Chris understood it pretty literally and that's just what he did, he left. Of course, he got a lot of help from that brownnoser over there, the Birkenstock artist."

"What's his deal?" Farah asked, conversational tigress that she is.

"Art, obviously. But if you want to commune with his inimitable works, don't waste your time and money on the subway. Take a couple of dirty Q-tips and use an Ikea pencil to draw a dick. And screw some patchy-bearded bigshot so he'll stand next to it repeating, 'Hm, an unusual collision of mature transmission and the infantile aesthetics of waste and scribbles,' or, 'The artist places regressive quotation marks around the traumatic experience of physical intimacy.'

"But stop me the moment I start nattering on about it again. This was supposed to be my No Chris Night. It's just that as soon as I say 'This is my wild fucking awesome No Chris Night' I immediately picture you-know-who, and it starts to be my not-fucking-awesome, lousy No Chris Night Only Let's Be Honest Chris Is There Night, that is, the worst, worst kind of evening that could happen to me. You want some? I've poured us some wine, a whole lot of people didn't finish theirs. We can't allow such wastefulness in Princetown when the price of alcohol has gone through the roof!"

Fah obediently drank up the several cups of not-so-refined booze with not-so-refined gulps. No fuss; it was a trick she'd been shown more than once by pirates downing 200 percent spirits from human skulls. All she knew was that she didn't at all want to go home, even if the bags under her eyes tomorrow get tangled in her legs on her way to work. You know those characteristic instances when you're hysterically holding on to some moment, not wanting to let it pass into the past: you want to record it, collect it, play it in a loop, never mind that any second now your tape deck is going to turn into a pumpkin, the cassette into a kohlrabi, and your swanky Sex Pistols T-shirt into a suet-stained dishrag.

Oh, if only Joanne could see her now! Laughing her ass off, or at least . . . laughing, chatting . . . well . . . listening . . . surrounded by . . . at any rate, *standing not far from* this bohemia. Her, poor stupid Farah; she'd simply burn up with envy! She'd shove the Hungarianist so far off the patio he'd roll down a precipice and right into the ocean, where the ravenous mermaids would tear him to shreds. They'd disappear into the nooks and wrecks of yachts, they'd while away the rest of the day fondling each other with his blackened arms. Whereas Joanne would turn her Pinto around and speed like a bat out of hell to be here, too, only . . . Too late, Joanne, you needed to have come up with this earlier.

"Have I told you about Chris and his——?" Go asked as they were leaving, but she was interrupted by a drawn-out hiccup. Meanwhile, from her handbag she had removed a measuring tape, a few old tickets, and a single-use sock for trying on shoes, all of which looked like a prestidigitator's trick. "Oh, hell, that son of a gun pissed in my bag!"

"What?" Farah followed up, having staggered around and caught the scent of cat pee.

It had suddenly gotten late, everyone had scampered off. Crumpled cups were scattered in front of the gallery. The neon signs of downtown were blaring somewhere off in the distance.

"So then: where do you live?"

"In Bath," Farah hiccupped.

"Bath?" Go hiccupped back, trying to catch a cab. "What street? I'll catch us a cab. I'm guessing you have no desire to rough it on those awful buses full of improbable homeless people and their old hangers?"

"Have I gone nuts?" Farah ventured to inquire. That was still the remains of her consciousness, the absolute dregs. A cab to Bath would cost at least seventy dollars. But Go is already hailing a yellow minivan, calmly eyeing her whose purse contained seventy cents, seventy gum wrappers, and seventy condoms, but that's all she had seventy of, and . . . and . . .

"To Bath," however, is what she's now saying to the cabbie, burping loudly. "I'll ride with you, I know some people nearby."

Saying this, she takes a ridiculously large straw hat with a veil that she'd gotten God knows where and plants it on her head. "I don't know what's come over me. I swiped it from that goofy show. It'll come in handy for this year's cotton harvest."

"And you, I'll warrant, will go in this," she says, wrapping her own fur collar around Fah's neck.

At which point she starts to cackle, to burst out laughing. Fah laughs for a minute longer with her, but . . . It suddenly occurs to her that she doesn't find it all that funny. Significantly less so, maybe even not at all! What, in fact, is this Go's deal? She's laughing at her, and Fah has the impression that this laughter is everywhere, that it's attacking her like a flock of seagulls does a defenseless old sandwich. Go

92

bares her rapacious little teeth, previously pearly white, now wine-stained black. She looks disgusting, like a child with rabies.

Fah no longer feels so happy, so delighted. She smells the nasty odor of upholstery and cat pee, she senses her own alienation. And, at the same time, a sort of longing for Go, who is sitting next to her, instead of it being Farah together with Farah and helping her take that damn antibacterial gel from her handbag. She looks at the refinery now passing by the taxi, and those lights are jumping in her eyes like small, still unborn frogs, and maybe they're just bacteria. A dead animal is sitting on her neck, in her mouth there's a bad aftertaste and diseases from some other people's mouths that have accumulated on her tongue in the form of a thick film. She really wants to spit, and what's worse, she might.

"I know I was taking it too far," Go is saying the whole time. "I know I loved him too much, terribly, obsessively, terribly, like no one ever has. So then why did he do it? Why did he leave me for that little shit? We live together, but he hates me like a dog, foremost because of my being from Poland. That's this country in the Former Yugoslavia, maybe you've heard of it. When I was really little, there was a total outbreak of communism there. My childhood was pretty messed up because of it. Maybe that's why I'm like this.

"You want to see my tattoo? Here. On my groin. An eagle. I don't know why I thought that would be the best place for it, it was an impulse. I go get a Brazilian, but I don't trust it. Each time I have the impression that the lady is pulling my whole pussy out by the roots. How are you doing? Is everything okay? Hello?"

"Yes," Farah whispers softly, maybe even inaudibly. She's

imagining a pussy's roots, which isn't at all pleasant. They're huge, overgrown, red; they reach deep, to suck up the juices; they send it everything, everything else.

"Look at these hands of mine," Go says, touching Farah's neck. "They're rough, it's because of Mr. Foods. Go's aunt's advice: never eat their mac'n'cheese. And in general: nothing that contains even a hint of béchamel. If you're already up to swallowing sperm, then only from people you know. And like, at least. Oh my, you're not about to . . . ???"

Stop the car! Stop the car!

CHAPTER 13

He shouldn't add so much to the fare. But that's Arabs for you. You almost only threw up on yourself, and right away he has to sanitize the whole upholstery and wash and buff the body! I told him I was going to report him to the Better Business Bureau. Oh, he can shove it up his ass. Money is so totally dated.

Church, churches are so romantic, wonderfully nonsensical. I'm going through a complete religious phase. I was a Buddhist, but isn't that becoming ordinary? Boredom like nobody's business—"Sorry, I'm off to my seclusion." From that they made something to supplement colon therapy. I'm starting to like church. The sullenness, the properness, the gilding, total madness. Only I can't motivate myself because on Sundays I always have the worst hangover. Though I don't truck with religious people not being able to use a rubber. It's sick: how are they supposed to protect themselves from AIDS?

But I adore the smell of a church; why don't they make perfumes like that? Incense, naphthalene, mold, and old man breath, it reminds me of childhood, that monstrous communism. It's always before my eyes, the image of me running in from the yard, out of breath, I open the fridge, I want to reach for the bottle of supercarbonated root beer, but all there is is a pitcher of moldy tea. Remember—we didn't have that other stuff! Our diet consisted almost exclusively of pierogi, borscht, kielbasa, and those rotten little pickles they had. And bootcakes. Don't ask me what that is, but I adore it, with melted butter. My parents were hardly ever home, they fought. Anyway, we all fought, we children helped too, as much as we could. Mama printed fliers calling on the people to boycott the system, she gave them to us, and my siblings and I handed them out at subway entrances, at shopping centers, at language schools. I walked out onto my balcony and looked through my binoculars at that whole Berlin Wall thing. People wanted to cross it, they came with ladders, tractors, but all for naught. It was enormously tall, and so airplanes kept getting snagged on it, and the clouds stopped on our side, and it was constantly raining, while in the West there was constantly sun.

So, as that brownnoser Chris now tells me . . .

Oh, I'm sorry, I start to fall apart whenever I get stoned . . .

Truth be told, I have nothing against him. I don't hate him in the obvious way any average person would in my shoes. I accept the fact that Chris is polyamorous, and that because of that I have to tolerate a person I don't tolerate, but that doesn't mean I'm not going to think the thing that's staring me right in the face. He's constantly undermining my person, he undermines what I say and do. He maintains that I'm upset. *I'm* upset, even though I've been going to therapy for four years! A single spark is enough, and we'll be at each other's throats. When we finally had it out, he got an earful of everything I think about him and his art, and I ran out. I bought a bottle of whiskey and got on the first subway car that came along. I was blind with rage, deaf! I screamed down the whole car, drinking. What, just because my boy-friend has suddenly become a fag out of nowhere, now he has to be with another one, too? Shitty queers. Finally, I went into some hairdresser's and ordered them to cut my hair down to the skin. I was in a sort of fugue state, I don't even know how I paid, because I didn't have a cent on me! And just then . . .

Hey, are you even still listening? Am I going on about this to myself?

Hello?

Holy moly, Farah, that couple of glasses totally did you in. I thought we'd drop in on these people I know who live over by the mall. But in the end it's as it always is: I'll go by myself. No, it's okay, after all, it's not your fault. Peace out, nice to meet you! But don't sit there blooming on this bench too long, because there's a ton of shady guys hang-ing around here.

CHAPTER 14

It was on just that Saturday morning that I saw her in the elevator.

We arrived in the morning; it was maybe eight; eight o'clock on a Saturday is like minus three in the morning on a normal day, the city's like an alcohol-sex bomb has gone off. Even the dogs can't be bothered to go out for a piss, because they don't want to step on the corpses in the bushes, the broken bottles and Preven packaging. Saturday mornings drive me into black depressions. The same as Sunday evenings, Monday lunches, and insistent Tuesday afternoons filled with the echo of wastebasketball, the cry of children, and the sound of "busy singles" listening to their recorded messages. One way or another, the real estate agent who was working with us maintained that showing us this apartment on days and hours that would be less idiotic was, as far as he was concerned, impossible. "And it would be a shame," he added. "It's an absolute gem; we barely got the listing."

Let's not bother about his name. But you know how it is when someone rubs you the wrong way right off the bat.

It's like they say not to judge a book by its cover, but on the other hand, why is it that it's sometimes enough to take one look at it, you know, sometimes maybe you have to add a quick glance at the title page or ISBN, but you know with complete certainty that you don't want to have this book, not even at the bottom of your basement? Not even at the bottom of *someone else's* basement? Not even to prop up the leg of the bookshelf?

All the tolerance, all the mental Food Not Bombs suddenly turns into a great big Bombs Bombs Bombs and No Fucking Food. You treat the dude to the blade of your mocking gaze, and your brain slips you little specks of as-if-innocent associations and impressions, from which you assemble neat subgroups of now slightly perfidious commentary. Nor will you examine yourself, but rather cobble together fraudulent, venom-saturated narratives regarding him, rife with sophisticated cruelties, frothing metaphors that classify his existence at the same level as shrimp, though at least shrimp are sometimes tasty . . .

"The panoramic window is something quite special," the poor, clueless guy woos, opening the stairwell door for us, while I'm wondering what animal he'll be reborn as. My bet was on a clever mouse, and I was looking forward to the moment when I'd share this deduction with Ernest. You could already see nature's first attempt at this incarnation. The lilac-colored shirt, matching scarf, the missing eyetooth, the remaining teeth similarly maintained, in the national colors of coffee and tea. The raven black of his Latin-dyed hair ruined by intervals of inadequately tended roots. Additionally, with his every gesture he endeavored to suggest his own absolute innocence and unimpeachable goodness. It's people like that who are the worst, in my opinion. In the smokescreens of his obsequious gestures, his fawning contortions, his financial-expert eyes were drilling into everything like two X-ray machines. It seemed like he could bring you to the point of vomiting with his obsequiousness. On the other hand, you could be sure that when you're not looking he'd put you up for auction on eBay and get a pretty good penny for your person, better than you are in any position to get for yourself!

"Careful, because this could make your head spin," he smiled mysteriously and bountifully, letting us in.

The apartment was like any other: empty space with traces of the furniture that had been moved out. A bit of dust, a scuffed leather sofa. Relatively okay, compared with some of the others we'd seen. Though the panorama stretched out before the window really was pretty rad. A decent-sized street below, and farther on, as complicated as the inside of a VCR, the whole of Bath took over, with its huge shopping center and multiplex, at this hour enveloped in morning mist, defenseless, deactivated. The opposite block of apartments, built strangely close somehow, obscured half of it, more or less; looking at this window, one already imagined smelling the specific stench of oil and rat poison.

"You'll really get down to writing with a view like this, eh?" the agent winked at me, pleased with his cleverness. He must have thrown our names into Google when we were filling out the application at the real estate office. He's sure to ask me for my autograph on his company notepad. He's the kind of guy who traipses around afterward telling people that he works with writers, who are gradually joined in his telling by painters, doctors, soldiers, so he can ultimately claim that he's found apartments in complexes for presidents, premiers, and the Dalai Lama . . .

"And then there's the espresso machine," he threw in uneasily, sensing the contemptuous look I'd cast at his pointy shoes. He even tried to turn it on, but the appliance, placed here merely to fill in the view, with a tremendous film of mold remaining in the filter, farted unreflectively and petered out, and he shrugged his shoulders.

"It reeks unbearably of roach powder," I said, *only* to Ernest.

"It's close to everything," he said placatingly, an incorrigible Mr. Let's-Just-Get-Along.

"Depends what your idea of 'everything' is," I said. "If it's a cheese shop and a baseball field, then yes."

"'Everything' to me means you have to write the damn book. We can't keep living out of cardboard boxes."

The agent withdrew. He had weakened a bit, disappointed by my brusqueness. He'd evidently hoped I'd like him and that I'd be haunted by the very recollection of his charming person. Surely he was imagining that when he went out I'd light a cigarette, looking dreamily out the window, and after that would take a typewriter out from under my coat and start writing.

"To think that this eloquent, fine specimen of a man was a real estate agent,"

or,

"Behind his eyes lurked an infinite cunning."

CHAPTER 15

Long story short: it wasn't possible. For a number of reasons.

I think that at my level of creative stimulation at the time I might perhaps have been capable of writing just the *To think*.

And then look at it for three hours, thinking to myself: shit, shit, shit, what decent book doesn't start with "to think"???

Or else I'd write only "Behind his eyes." And cut it off immediately. I'd stare at the laptop screen saying "behind his eyes" to myself—that's fine for Michael Allen, he's as big a hack as they come, he drinks, he has a stupid haircut, and he's already published his third book in two years . . .

At the time I was suffering from a most spiteful case of creative constipation. And though I tried various ways of psyching myself up for work, it was like trying to walk through a wall: the more force and ferocity you put into it, the more suffering it brings. I was ultimately sure to close Word and throw myself on the couch, and my bitter sighs would make even a dead man feel guilty. It was sure to provoke one of those conversations with Ernest, typical of this last month, about the pitifully foreseen things to come.

•

"What's going on?" he'd ask without tearing his eyes from his laptop.

"Nothing's going on. It's nonsense."

"In what sense?" Ernest'd ask, treading the unsteady ground of his divided attention.

"In no sense," I'd shoot back, the tears already welling in my eyes. "This whole book's a clusterfuck."

"You can't think that way," he'd say. "You can't know that until you've written it."

"What do you mean by that?" I'd ask, passably neutrally. But only to allow him to discern the avalanche gathering within me.

"I mean that once you write it, you'll be able—"

"So what do you suggest?" I'd spring up, performing a gesture of desperation I'd seen on some TV show. "What else am I doing all day? You think I sit in front of a blank page browsing Facebook? Or that I wander aimlessly around town? Is that what you're getting at? Well, maybe I do. What's more, it's true! And do you know why that is? Because I have no inspiration. We're too close. I'm suffocating, we're practically sitting on each other's head! Because of you I'm censoring myself, I'm falsifying reality so that what I write won't be quite so painful to you!"

Smelling the fumes of absurdity starting to waft in all around me, I'd make an effort to inflect my screams with a conciliatory/common-sense tone.

"Obviously, don't take this the wrong way. I don't mean that the fact I can't write is your fault. You have nothing to do with it, it's simply that you distract me. That's just how you are, there's too much of you. Too much of you and your constant blah blah blah and all your papers; just look at it in here! When you take out a DVD, you never put it back in its place. There's a different disc in every case. I reach for Antonioni, inside it's Fellini. I reach for Woody Allen, inside it's Pasolini. I know, I know you're trying not to make any noise. But that doesn't help! It makes everything even worse. Those contortions, your soundlessly setting the mug on the coffee table. This whole ballet you're constantly doing in here: tiptoeing around, leaving the door ajar! I cannot write under these conditions! The noise! Our neighbors talk too loud. The air-conditioning growls. The stuffiness. The atmospheric pressure. The constant echoes of the elevator. Social problems. Corporations. PMS. The end of civilization!"

Before my tirade would finally stop resounding in one of those nightmarish apartments we quit after a month in order to look for the next, I already knew I'd regret it. It's my nature. Never get involved with people who write: it's unbearable. They blow up in hysterics, they torment, they fire at random, whoever they come across goes to the woodshed. They pump out words en masse and without a care, like they were knitting clothes out of air, just to knit, just to assemble them into somehow decent shapes, into stunning cakes layered with bile and tar. Whereupon, having adorned them with the final touch of asbestos icing, the last drop of venom, and a cyanide cherry, they recoil, they freeze, terrified, devastated by themselves, by their own wickedness.

It was the same thing with this real estate agent: after calling him every name in the book in my head, I was seized by pangs of conscience. I started to feel terribly sorry. Maybe he wasn't evil, maybe he was as innocent as a babe, an unhappy little man with exposed roots and pointy shoes saying "this window" and "this traffic circle" and "not in the least" instead of "at least"; he didn't need to add my disdain to the collection of his hopelessness. For this reason I had a hangover, and I suddenly wanted to give away the entire advance on the book, all my savings, to shelters for rabid dogs. Because I figured that at this rate I'm going to be reborn as one of them, and that I have to make advance arrangements for the conditions in which I would have to live.

"Well then, we're going to think it over," Ernest was still saying to him, smiling apologetically as we were leaving that apartment. As usual, he felt foolish for me. "It's a serious decision, my partner is just now in the middle of working on . . ." His words were drowned out by the elevator I had called, which was now arriving with a wheeze. I briskly opened the door and . . . It'll be shortest if I say that some girl was sitting on the floor of the elevator.

Sitting is overstating it. Her limbs were somewhat twisted and cast all around, totally as if the gigantic baby girl-mutant that had been playing with her a moment earlier and was called to lunch by her nursemaid had suddenly flung her into a corner and run off, obstructing the sidewalks and snagging ribbons on the buildings.

The craters left by her bootees were surely still steaming.

"Maybe we'll take the stairs, then," the agent said, fixing his eyes on the vomitus randomly smeared on her skirt. Beside her lay a wilted handbag that, as if not wanting to leave its owner in a lurch, had also vomited up a wave of trinkets to keep her company.

"We'll fit," I said, planting careful steps among the ragged, as if waterlogged, issue of *Yogalife* and the silver card from a yoga club.

"*Farah,*" Ernest read off the card.
"Farah Fatset," I contributed.
And the elevator moved.

CHAPTER 16

How did they know her name?

Farah opened a distrustful dormer through her eyelid and saw only some oaf with a dye-job and a missing eyetooth. He was the one who'd been patting her on the shoulder for quite some time, saying, "Can I help you, ma'am?" and just for kicks lifting her hand, which fell inertly.

"She'll be fine," he said stupidly when she finally shoved his hand away with disgust. "She's alive, right?"

There were two other people there whom she had never seen before: a dude and a woman. No, she didn't know them. Maybe they had dropped in at "Trash Hospital" too? Maybe they'd even bought themselves an old trench coat sleeve to hang in the living room?

She was, without a doubt, in an elevator. Why did she come to this whole gallery opening in an elevator? And how? How had she fit it into the bus? Never mind. It was certainly *madly original*, but it was at least two times more confounding still. She had so many things to say, utterly witty, and if they would just let her concentrate, if they weren't standing over her like this . . .

•

The elevator dropped and stopped, there was a shuffling of shoes, and those people got out. Then it turned out that they'd rented an apartment on that entryway; she saw them a few days later as they were bringing in cardboard boxes, and she avoided their gaze.

"Hey," she was still trying to yell after them now. "I live here too! We can be friends and have pillow fights!" But then she smelled her own breath and immediately understood that that's why they'd gone: her mouth smelled something awful.

Neat freaks!

And so what if she bought her breath in one of the secondhand shops on St. Patrick's, huh? The one where they sell those messed-up hipsters getups from the "bad-as-it-is, it-can-always-be-even-worse" line? So what that she'd stopped by the little rack and, from among the unusual flavors of gum—"Just-Eaten Head of Garlic Chomped with a Bit of Onion," "Lamb Shawarma Eaten Two Days Ago"— what she had chosen was "Half-Digested Whiskey, Cigarettes, Stomach Acid, and Too Shit-Faced to Use Listerine"???

Then she put more in her basket, some "Superman," a bit of scabies, and silicon blister pads . . . "Poor Woman on a Pilgrimage": that's apparently the hottest style this season. To that she added the cover of *The Sermons of Piotr Skarga*, whatever that was, made out of rubber. A wacky gadget— maybe she'd put it on some random book and spend the afternoon at Bad Berry sipping an eight-buck soy latte and, from behind her Ray-Bans, fish for the gazes of all those kindly prisoners of their own predictability . . .

A sure thing: at last no one, truly *no one* knows what's up with you. And Bad Berry really is trendy these days. They have slow-pressed espresso for dogs and little tables where dogs can sit down with their MacBooks. It's all the rage: they only have, like, three letters on their keyboard (W, O, and F), but they have Firefox like everybody else, and in his free time, when he's not playing, studying, or shopping, your dog can watch clips on YouTube, show them to other dogs, they can have parties where they watch them together (buddy, haven't you seen this?) (no, no, I have a better one to show you), they have a cool design in general, they get fewer viruses, and her dog is really much happier with it than he had been with the PC he'd had before.

Farah stood up, supporting herself against the elevator's wall with drunken haughtiness, and started gathering her things, woefully scattered like her entire being, into her handbag.

CHAPTER 17

She felt horrible.

Who wouldn't feel horrible? It was all wrong! "All is lost!" she sniveled, knocking over the objects on the kitchen counter. The little teapot, the granulated fiber, the milk thistle, the turbo-stewer that she'd lied to Joanne about, saying it was Ingeborg who'd bought it straight from that parasite doctor . . . When she had bought it herself! Yes, herself! Hangover anguish, like a tightly wound streamer, was merely awaiting an object around which it might spew all its colors, curlicues, fireworks. Yes, she had been lying back then, telling Joanne about that doctor who treated his patients with a ski pole! She'd been to see him herself! Twice at that!

She'd lost it all. Not long ago she'd been with Go and was having a pretty good time. They were friends, one might be so bold to say! She had someone close, someone who wants her, accepts her, and even touches her! Now she had nothing. In her bag—not a trace of anything. Other than antibacterial gels and a couple other pieces of garbage. No token, no business card, no piece of paper with a number. The only things left to her were her bacteria-covered hands and the awful pain that had found itself a cozy little spot in her head and, having curled up into a hard, hot ball, was splitting her temples. In an impatient and system-free manner she riffled through the medicaments in the cabinet searching for a sachet of Theraflu Sinus. She didn't have time for hours-long negotiations, for playing hide-and-seek; she could play only find, and now, immediately, otherwise she'd be forced to smash her head with a vase or other heavy object, but her skills at self-destruction haven't yet reached such an advanced level. She won't know how to do it discreetly enough not to leave traces, for it to go unnoticed at work.

Suddenly, at lunch on Monday, a piece of her forehead would fall into her arugula salad.

"Is everything alright, Farah?" Ingeborg would ask, disconcerted, trying to help her fish the bone out from among salad leaves and cherry tomatoes.

"It's no big deal," Farah would say, avoiding her gaze, hastily brushing the vinaigrette from her forehead and stuffing it back into place. "It's chronic forehead wasting disease; I've suffered from it since childhood."

When she had succeeded in jamming it into place, however, the back of her head, stuck on with duct tape, would pop off, and the randomly curled folds of her brain would pour out like a garden hose right at the feet of the screaming Ingeborg and down beneath the Xerox machine. All her thoughts would sprinkle and spurt out, her obsessions, every molecule of her psyche, a microscopic Joanne hysterically clutching a tube of glue, the Hungarianist a lavatory sign, her mother a prescription from the ear-nose-throat doctor, Go with a French fry, Ingeborg with a binding machine, and at the very end an itty-bitty Farah who miraculously succeeds in crawling into a pack of Theraflu Sinus, thanks to which . . .

•

With what is left of her strength she sprinkles it into a glass and, adding water from the tap, is now quite close to salvation. But just then the doorbell rings.

Farah sets the glass aside. It's the pill-popping first-floor neighbor. His body language expresses worry and inhibition, but also excitement. He's shaved, as the numerous nicks, irritations, and remnants of lather on his jowly cheeks attest. A neat part separates his thinning hair into equal halves, which comes to twenty hairs on each side, gelled to the skin along their entire length, just in case (those bothersome drafts!). His legs, thick as two tree stumps, stick out of skateboard sneakers. He's keeping his hands folded ostentatiously at his lap, like someone who's ready to get down to business.

"Hi," he says, like it's all good.

"Hi," Farah replies, shielding herself behind the door. "Where did you get that?" she almost screams, suddenly spotting her birth control pills in his hand.

"What?"

"That!"

"Can I come in for a minute? I have a problem."

"What problem?!"

Maybe it's the end of the world? She sort of even wished it were. She had too little strength not to let him in, she could have been talked into anything at this point. ("Would you give us your identity?" a nice volunteer from Identity Bank, Inc., could have asked her now. "Those who donate also receive a substitute identity, a cute 'Identimouse' plush toy, and a shirt with our fund drive logo."

"Sure . . . why not?" Farah would answer, signing the consent for the operation and indemnifying them in case of death, examining the swag she'd received with a dull eye. Why are free T-shirts always Larges? No big deal, she'll turn it into dustrags.)

She hobbled to the kitchen and knocked back the glass of medicine. She squinted; sunlight that would take no guff fell in through the window. The boy toddled in after her, looking everything over as if wondering where best to install the smoke detectors.

"They were in the elevator," he said, setting the pills on the counter. His hands, with their stubby little fingers and chewed-up fingernails, recalled the paws of some creature of the abyss. "I thought they were yours."

"*They're not mine,*" she said, in all caps.

"That's okay. Because you shouldn't take them anymore."

"Why not?"

"They're expired!"

"So what?" Farah screamed, tossing them theatrically into the garbage. Actually, trying to toss them in.

"This too," he said, taking antibacterial gel from this pocket. "Did you get shit-faced?"

"Why?"

"Because you have puke on your skirt."

Farah glanced down and almost burst into tears.

"I shouldn't talk like that, I'm sorry," he retreated, helpless before her dejection.

"That has nothing to do with me."

"I've made you uneasy. You look uneasy."

"I'm not uneasy!"

"It's actually an intimate matter. You could have something with your stomach."

113

"Not at all! Let's just drop it."

"No, no, really. I myself hate when somebody asks me lots of questions. Just like my Aunt Peg does on the holidays. 'How are those growths on your testicles doing, Albert?' 'They've gotten even bigger, Aunt Peg, now I can barely button my pants. They totally don't fit in the legs.' And so on."

"Stop!!!"

"It's horrible, don't laugh."

"I'm not laughing, in case you didn't notice! I have a cough."

"I'm Albert."

"I have allergies."

"You mean I should go?"

"If only."

"Too bad."

"Really too bad."

"You could tell me."

"I am telling you."

"But I can't leave without giving this back to you," he said, and from the pocket of his trunks he pulled that ruddy fur collar that Go had wound around her yesterday. "What?" he lamented. "It was lying in the elevator!"

She snatched the collar and locked the door, loudly, all the locks. Albert smelled like teenagers at their first disco: perfume applied beyond all moderation, the quantity of which totally doesn't even allow eventual talk of quality.

Go's collar carried the label Zach de Boom and must have been either terribly expensive or, at the very least, difficult to steal.

CHAPTER 18

Remember that episode of *Little House on the Prairie* where Laura Ingalls finds an injured fox in the woods and offers it her bonnet? Despite knowing that they're not making ends meet, and that on account of this she'll probably have to wear a wicker basket on her head all winter?

When she has a hangover, whether she wants to or not, a person always starts thinking about such things. She'd like to spill tears—no, to open the window and roar for the entire street, but then she thinks that Laura is so good and pure that such a repulsive, vodka-reeking stinker isn't even worthy of crying for her.

That's how things were now. A cool but sunny afternoon was hanging idly out the window, empty as a balloon; Fah was lying on the unpleasantly warm bedsheets, and her heartbeat was weak, like an infant's breathing.

The crazy evening appeared as its own kind of sliced-up and markedly incomplete cinematic material that ran alternately in two versions. One told the story of her and Go. In it they were running hand in hand to the other side of the rainbow, to throw themselves on the grass and smother each other in kisses, and in the meantime let the remaining six billion people do as they please.

This version overwhelmed her body with a sweet joy not often found in her heart, and then with desire and longing. So, for the sake of balance, a second version appeared, assembled from shots that hadn't made it into the first. In it, Farah, totally drunk, rejected the vertical posture common to the human species in favor of the horizontal, while she replaced the traditional gait with a less effective, but more affecting, or at least attention-grabbing one: crawling, creeping, slithering, and sliding in her own vomit. With her slapstick debasement she erased any chance at Go's friendship, any chance of anything, of *anything* else, whatever it might be.

The worst thing was that she was unable to decide unequivocally on one version or the other. In a paradoxical sort of way, she believed in both at the same time, she wasn't sure of anything, and, in the end, just like that, she was staring blankly at her phone, as if looking at it long and hard enough could make Go call her.

But she did not call.

Neither that weekend, nor after.

How loathsome the silence seems, how worthless the trinkets on the shelves, how boring, how infinitely boring her work. How the great futility and superficiality of our existence descend upon us when for a moment someone shows us a life that's colorful, crazy, it'll beguile us with its hues, it'll tickle us with its sensual proximity, it promises a coupon for everything that's missing, so that . . .

So that it suddenly disappears, leaving us to prey upon ourselves. We're like a starving boy who doesn't yet know life, to whom a derelict will show a dirty leaflet in some corner. A card with some legs-spread babe whose anus has been first displayed, then covered by a computerized star. We're disgusted, we don't know what to do first: throw up or put our hands over our eyes, and finally we decide on the latter, leaving a bit of space, however, between our fingers, so as not to miss out on any of the image's enticing nastiness. Whereas afterward, infected with this impure sweetness or, if you prefer, this sweet impurity, we lie there through sleepless nights, craving something, longing for something, trying to be attracted to something.

That's how Farah was lying. That's how she spent her time at work. Her timid investigation, executed with trembling hands, brought certain results. On Google she found what you might expect if you do a search for "Go." On the page for the Lizard's Stomach, perhaps rarely updated, there was an invitation to a lecture from three months ago. At the site for Mr. Foods, under the "Our Team" tab, she discovered handy information for those applying to be members of the wacky Mr. Foods crew ("Give It a Shot!"). In her inbox, vacation pics from Joanne, which she didn't even open. She was looking out the window of the offices of Bloch & Geek, behind which the city was buzzing, busy and boundless. Human waves flowing in and out of the subway, spilling through the subterranean walkways, building up into transitory masses at their entrances, swelling in the squares, only to disperse again a moment later in the side streets into which Go vanished like a bikini top in the ocean—now you'll never find her, never, never!

And at that thought she started banging her wrists against the edge of whatever, till they went reddish, and then she had to wear blouses with long sleeves. Having pulled them down all the way to her fingers, she listened to the discussions regarding the plan for the latest campaign. To her they seemed like the rustle of a distant garbage dump that hipsters wandered in search of fur collars and badass wall lamps, and from the tossed-out sandwiches the gulls ate only the Parma ham, skipping the rest, because they're none too fond of romaine, and that goes double for Dijon . . .

CHAPTER 19

Finally, she resolved to act.

On Wednesday after work she boarded the G Line, which runs to St. Patrick's.

Have you ever been there? It's this great big postindustrial district on the river dominated by a variety of emigrants who don't exactly gush individual happiness. Anyway, some of you are sure to live there, right, it's the thing now . . . To me it will always be one of those neighborhoods about which people are constantly saying that "in light of the low rents more and more artists are setting up studios and galleries here," "many clubs with an artistic flair are popping up here," "given the large number of artists, we have a lot of artists here," and other hogwash from real estate agents who want to get hysterical snobs into the damp local apartments, with their broken blinds and mild fecal odor.

"They'll write about you in *Yogalife,* in their *Home* insert! You'll be able to show the exposed brick interior, the bath mat made from recycled bottle caps, and the house mold made from genuine mold!" Meanwhile, in every other store window, next to the ring of sausage, there's actually an ad for bedbug removal, and the majority of stores are junk shops offering teapot stands, defunct fax machines, busted angle joints, slightly broken yet still functional "Return" and "Option" keys for an Atari 64, dresses with yellow armpits, and a one-of-a-kind collected works of Shakespeare from the seventeenth century without a cover, spine, or pages. On the other hand, I know folks who maintain that there's really no shortage of good pubs around here, and it's a good place to spend quite pleasant, lazy Sundays. Around noon you can pounce on *g-noke-chee* with Brazil-nut sauce, Thai risotto with raspberries, and biolamb-and-pesto sandwiches, and afterward bum around till five, stuffed and bloated, sipping a mojito, giggling, and making up dialogue for the winos tussling with the garbage cans.

Yum, I adore gnocchi.

Obviously, in such places you certainly do not expect to find a Mr. Foods, where Go said she works. And at the counter of which Fah was now standing, sweating and pretending to be reading the menu, held at the business end of a robust black woman's disgruntled gaze. No, it was quite certain that the interiors there had not been designed by Guy MacFerry, they didn't have curtains in a Kim Gordon pattern, the lavatory was not wallpapered in *Kama Sutra,* and they didn't import the meat from a farm outside of Portland where the animals are allowed to have tape decks in their room and the right to speak with a psychologist before they die.

Mr. Foods turned out to be a decent-sized, crowded, poorly air-conditioned dive whose clientele is recruited from among food decadents subconsciously attempting to commit suicide by unchecked ingestion of cholesterol. You could see it in the menu, full of such lethal atrocities as "Fifteen Cheese Spaghetti," "Fried Snickers with a Rad Mars Puree," and "Nugget-Breaded Chicken Wings." There was also a ratty bar, a clogged toilet seething with old maxi pads, and a backyard area where stray dogs scraped through Styrofoam containers of leftovers.

"I'll have . . ." Farah said. "I'll have . . . I'll have a large nuggets."

"We don't do Large."

"What kind do you do?"

"We have Huge, Gigantic, and Monstrous."

"Huge, then."

"Extra fat?" the cashier asks.

"No, without extra fat."

"Do you want an extra fifteen hundred calories for a buck fifty?"

"No, thank you."

"Quadruple or sextuple fries?"

"Quadruple."

"Thank you for your order."

No, no, I'm kidding, nothing of the kind ever took place.

"This is stupid, but . . . I'm looking for someone in particular," Farah said to the black woman.

Under the old-fashioned net the wads of her hair looked like bad fortunes from Chinese cookies.

"Her name's Go."

"Not here," she answered, seeking out the next customer with her eyes.

"And when will she be?"

"She hasn't been in at all this week."

"Would you give me a number where I could reach her?"

"I'm not allowed to give out information about other employees."

"Can I leave something for her?"

The black woman scooped the business card (upon which one could see the Bloch & Geek logo, and upon which Farah had written *Lizard's Stomach/last Friday*) contemptuously into the register, after which her whole corporeal being gave Farah to understand that she'd long since been serving other customers, and Farah was still just casting glances at the young people packing up Micknuggets. *How funny they are, lolling around in their aprons,* she thought, aching with envy, staring as they laughingly swapped French fries. Like in some TV show, *Whole Heap o' Trouble*, or *Honey, I Sank the Sinks*, surely everyone has a funny foible or one funny catchphrase. Fah, too, could quit her damned job at the agency, toss out the Zara outfit that pinched under the armpits, and join up with them, drizzling herself with greasy dishcloth water, playing pickle in the middle with a spit of shawarma, and blowing her wad in the macaroni for kicks . . .

Especially since dark clouds had been gathering over her at the agency. It was hard to hide so drastic a decline in her devotion to work, and by now it was totally hard, even without trying. For quarter hours at a time she'd wander around the office with a ream of copy paper on her shoulders, stumbling over the extension cords. Her absent gaze would slide over PowerPoints, the dust-covered blinds, the open MacBooks. Over the Prada labels affixed in symbolic quantities to eyeglasses, from behind which her colleagues would cast their own suspicious gazes upon her.

CHAPTER 20

"Is it the girl with the bloody pants again?"

The portly old mermaid pushed up her sliding Ray-Bans with just the one lens, through which one of her eyes appeared curiously larger than the other. It was all the more obvious that she no longer believed in anything and now wouldn't have anything against kicking the bucket. In the chipped ashtray she had a few fish skeletons whose heads she'd suck on gloomily from time to time. A bunch of wilted tulips was drooping from a bottle of Chlorine-Free Tide. She was leafing through, or rather holding upside down, a sodden issue of *Yogalife*. She knew only a few letters, yet she delighted in this atmosphere, the chic that a newspaper always affords.

"My eyes have grown tired," she told Farah, summoning her with a crooked finger. "You could read to me."

"'It's not discussed openly, because it's morally controversial,'" Farah read obediently, perched on a rust-eaten food processor. "'But among the wealthy inhabitants of countries in the West there is a growing mass of spiritual invalids who are ready to pay astronomical sums to no longer be themselves.' Should I keep reading?"

•

The other one just nodded, having sprawled comfortably on a platform of boards, upon which her great, greasy, worn-out tail lay paralyzed. This is how she got around, ever since she had been brutally beaten by the stoned passengers aboard some yacht—she couldn't swim on her own. The platform had been patched together from the bottom of some wardrobe or a scrap of theater stage and was outfitted with wheels from baby carriages, at least several different kinds, so that the whole vehicle wobbled and got mired in sand again and again. The world of mermaids, free of men, could not boast an advanced technical knowledge.

"'The perspectives that guide them are various,'" Farah read. "'Whether it's the enormity of the evil and abomination they've committed, which they are constantly reminded of, or else their protracted depression and feeling of unproductivity, their addiction to alcohol, narcotics, or an eating disorder. Not infrequently, applicants are motivated by sensual or sexual overindulgence, which has rendered them insensitive to stimuli and doesn't allow them to enjoy anything anymore. In India, where the law is unique in allowing this procedure, there are specialized clinics, shabby by Western standards, where they perform a very complex *ego transplant*. Though nothing is yet known regarding the moral aspect of this phenomenon, it is increasingly popular and brings mutual benefits to the clients, who most often are . . .'"

"Hold on," the old mermaid commanded, and she fell into a coughing fit. She must have gotten a bone stuck where it shouldn't be, because she was choking for a good long while. Farah read on, because the article interested her greatly—perhaps she'd like such an operation herself?

"'What's the problem, if it means these people are capable of enjoying their lives again—what's wrong with that?' Charlie, the actor famous for his Hollywood excesses, and whom everyone had already written off, answers the question with a question. Thanks to the operation, he's once again able to go on living, and his loved ones affirm that he's gradually returning to form. They say he's starting to enjoy tastes and smells, though he himself admits that his character has changed a bit. He's more panicky, tearful, he avoids intercourse with his partners and has started watching more TV.

"'Now the one battling his sex addiction, alcoholism, and drug dependency is the nineteen-year-old Nidhi, who doesn't have too many opportunities to give in to temptation on that score. She's gloomy and cries out in her sleep, she dreams of watermelon-like, juice-dripping ladies' crotches landing on her face, of washing her bits in Moët, of sex with overdeveloped teens dressed up as 'Little Pilgrim Girl,' but, as the courageous Nidhi attests, you can survive all of this . . . Silent suffering, internal emptiness, and the incapacity to enjoy anything—they were worth the four thousand euros she'd thus earned, and which enable her to send her four children to school.'"

"The End," Farah contributed, and the mermaid only smacked her lips melancholically, offering no comment on the article, maybe she hadn't understood much of it. She looked, God have mercy, like those salesgirls in the Yugoslav sausage shops. Her hair, gray, sparse, and ratty, was pinned to the top of her head with a child's Bugs Bunny clip; her eyelashes were covered in blue mascara, her facial features waterlogged and indistinct.

"Let's say I could help you find her," she said from out of nowhere, tossing fish skeletons onto the mountain of trash and examining Farah unsympathetically.

"Who?"

"Don't be dumber than you are, little girl."

"Really, could you . . . ?" Farah asked.

"Let's say I could."

"How?"

"Don't worry about how. Worry about how much it'll cost."

"I can pay you," Farah said.

"Huh," the mermaid blurted.

"I can give you my DVD player."

"I have a DVD player," the mermaid said. "It doesn't work in the water. I want . . ."

"Yes?" Farah asked, already aware that whatever it was, it was going to be expensive.

"I want your hair."

"Sorry?!"

"Believe me, mine used to be beautiful, too. But you can't maintain beautiful hair in such contaminated water. You'd see that yourself soon enough. It thins out, falls out, until finally it become like a dishtowel. So maybe you'll say it's too high a price. But I thought this was just something you really cared about."

Did she still have a choice? Maybe she did, perhaps that's why she was crying so, wrapping her fingers around the rusty scissors.

CHAPTER 21

Suddenly the alarm clock went off, violent and unrelenting.

The ocean tossed Farah onto the shore like a crippled castaway.

The cool, quiet monument of morning crumbled, blown apart by the as yet infrequent horns, the growling of buses, the taxis, which in about an hour should build into the everyday inferno. People extracted themselves from doorways, trailing purple lines of perfume in the air. IndiaVegeMan was already pumping out toxic clouds of curry that would brook no resistance, and that fell through the window with the broken blinds right into Fah's nose, where they left a greasy film.

I don't know whether this rings a bell, it's never happened to me personally, but it seems that some people have it like this all the time. You get up, none too pleased, things aren't going so great in your life. You drag your feet into the kitchen to put on the coffee . . . or else—same difference—to brew antiparasitic herbs in the turbo-stewer. There, kind of by accident, your gaze alights upon the floor, because there you see this sort of . . . This sort of, no two ways about it . . . Ultimately, the fact is it's no big deal, it doesn't matter how strange and unsettling it might be, specifically, that . . . To put it bluntly: hair. Your hair!

Well, maybe not all of it, let's just say: a decent amount. The first thing you do is grab your head, rush to the bathroom, in the meantime you find the rest of your hair on the floor . . . Your head looks like it's been through showers of acid rain, but you can't hold that against yourself: even the hairstyling masters don't always get it to come out straight when they're trimming their own hair in their sleep with their eyes closed. She was rummaging through her dresser in her hysteria, wondering how to cover it up. What was she to do? Call Joanne? Discreetly tease out whether she'd come back yet? Because there was no way she was taking this to the hairdresser. What would she say had happened to that hair of hers? A dog ate it?

"Farah?" Ingeborg asked at the agency with a sort of anxiety-provoking delicacy. Her mindless blue eyes, as though against her will, were following the droplets of sweat flowing out from under F's woolen cap. "Are you going to lunch?"

"Thanks, but I'm not really hungry," Fah said.

"Great, then it all works out," Ingeborg smiled self-consciously. "The boss wants to see you in his office."

CHAPTER 22

"For Tip-Tap faucets, Tip-Tap faucets," I was humming to myself as I was coming into the entryway, "get your faucets at Tip-Tap." Sometimes when I hear that song I hum it for so long that everybody wants to break off all contact with me. And after, when the little bells roll out and this guy comes in: "Your Housewares Depot, open *all week*." The pride in his voice!

I was bringing in a few boxes from the last apartment. It was quite a warm afternoon.

"Hey there, you don't happen to know whether Farah lives on this entryway?" I was asked by a tiny, bald-headed girl waiting at the elevator. The huge dark glasses, the cigarette behind the ear, the appallingly extravagant shoes, and the "tell me or you die" tone betrayed the chic of the affected youths of St. Patrick's. Beyond that, in one hand she held two huge H&M bags stuffed to the brim, in the other a cage with some shrieking creature and a gallon of Clorox for good measure.

"Farah?" I repeated, staring at these surprising personal effects. That's what the drunk from the elevator was called, the yoga girl. "I think so. But I don't know what floor. We've only just moved in."

"Oh, so I'm not the only one. I'm just moving in, too. Don't worry about the Clorox," she added. "I figured, I bought it, I'm taking it, because I'm the one who bought it, right? I'm not going to let a fuckhead like that use my bleach. Thanks," she said as I held the door for her. "Would you press three for me? My boyfriend really pissed me off. Or rather: my boyfriend, and his boyfriend. The vagaries of sexual postmodernism. Or call it what you want. Though at first it seemed like I accepted his polyamory. Well guess what: I don't. Oh, here we are. Goodbye."

She removed her glasses. She had mascara smeared all over her face.

"Long time no see," she said, and she sniffled.

"Long time no see," Farah muttered, hiding her trembling hands behind her back.

"Are you alone?" Go asked, lowering her small, beautifully rounded skull like a flag. "I didn't have anyone else to call."

With a reddened nose, dressed in jeans and an undershirt, it was as though in her hurry she hadn't managed to dive into the donated clothes bin. Tangible, genuine, real. No costume, no mask, no smokescreen of squeals and loud laughter, helplessly nibbling at her cuticles. She had called quite suddenly, out of nowhere, you could hear her choking back tears. "We have to talk," "You'll never guess what happened," "Can we meet?"

"I can come to you," Farah said, mortified, solemn, ready to make the highest sacrifices.

"No, no, I'm the one calling, I'll come to your place."

"It would be easier," Farah reassured her, glancing around her apartment, which suddenly seemed utterly pathetic, inadequate. "Stay where you are, and I'll come to you."

"You don't have to. I'm by the subway now."

Damn it! She only had a moment to change everything. To even out her hacked hair, shave her legs, come up with some questions, some jokes, amusing comments that she might then sprinkle in spontaneously. To mask various proofs of her being this awful her in spite of herself, to cram her life's most compromising traces into the coat closet—everything that could suggest that she has these various embarrassing afflictions: the metamorphosis of her matter, her feet, her nails, her teeth . . . Her legs buckled beneath her; her heart was pounding, pumping vanilla-heroin-swirl ice cream into her bloodstream, where it mixed with what had already been teeming therein, the distrust, the dread, the nerve-shot nausea, her lack of hair, and . . .

"This fatass a friend of yours?" Go asked as she came in.

. . . and the added shock of seeing Albert, the junkie who happened to be hanging around the garbage chute and, now that he'd been noticed, started pretending he was engrossed in reading the notice affixed to it.

"He's just some nutcase!" Farah said, locking the door behind her. "Perhaps he's in love with me."

"Where can I put my Clorox?"

"Wherever. It's a terrible mess in here."

"Sorry to drop in on you like this," Go said, looking around the apartment, dead and empty like an Ikea display room.

Dressed relatively normal, she had unusual distressed-fabric shoes on her feet. Neither pumps nor orthopedic sandals, they might have cost a thousand dollars, but they were so ugly you could easily figure that minus a thousand dollars would be quite a reasonable price as well.

"Don't worry about it!" Farah smiled warmly. "You really helped me out, too, that last time."

Go looked at her like she was a moron.

"You know, that time at the Lizard's . . . I was totally unconscious . . . and so forth," Farah stammered, blushing all over. She reached for the *Yogalife* she'd tossed open on the armchair a moment earlier, for show, and pretended to be leafing through it with great interest.

"I broke up with Chris," Go threw in, lighting a cigarette. "I know we broke up before, but now it's definite. I moved out."

"I got time off today," F. said, as though it were something quite comparable.

"It's over." Go made a melancholic inspection of her pedicure.

"My boss has determined that I'm overstrained. Seems the employees have noted strange behaviors and a general *decline in productivity*."

"Are you going to go somewhere?" Go asked hopefully. "If you do go away, I could look after your apartment for you."

"I haven't thought about going yet, but . . ."

"A week or two, I could stay here for you."

". . . I doubt it'll work out. They ordered me to attend a workshop for self-aggression."

"For what?"

"For sel— . . . for stress."

133

"Blow it off."

"I have to get a certificate of attendance."

"Oh, fine then! As always: Go, if you want to count on somebody, count on yourself!" Go sighed meaningfully as she opened the pantry. "Fine, I get it. Where do you keep your dishes? I have a present for you."

Farah's face dropped at the very sight of the Ballantine's, which Go poured herself a full glass of before adding a smidgen of Coke.

"You're not drinking?" she asked, blowing her nose.

"Thanks, but after the last time . . ."

"I have to, I totally have the shakes. And this is my cat."

"Cute," Farah said without touching him (parasites). He was an alley cat with a white ruff.

"I found him recently at a gallery. He was walking along the ledge and had no fucks to give. On the seventeenth floor! All I did was look at him and I knew he was like me, it was destiny. His name's Little Bastard. Chris and I thought of him as our child. Well, you Little Bastard, have a look around, don't be afraid. This is Auntie Farah!"

Farah looked at him with something that she imagined to be sympathy.

"I felt dumb for calling you—we hardly know each other." Go released the cat, which darted under the sofa. "But you understand. First I went to my friend's so she'd take care of me. But no dice. Sorry, Charlie."

"I understand you perfectly," Farah said. "My friend, when I was—"

"That's how people are! When I got there, she had just taken her morning-after pill. Her stomach hurt, and she had some bleeding down there. When I came in, she didn't even feel like getting out of bed! I had to make the tea for myself, look through her cabinets for something to take the edge off, all by myself, and all she did was lie there and moan. When I'm all shakes, I can't help myself, even a 'hand me a blanket, hand me that,' I'm no sister of mercy when I'm in such a state. Besides, she kept nattering on and on about being allergic to cats, and to prove it she started ostentatiously blowing her nose and sneezing. Now that was a cold, at the least. I told her, 'You can't do this to me, goddammit, you're my last lifeline. I told those two I was moving out once and for all, that I was taking the Little Bastard, it was all over, it was definite. I can't go back now.' But she just moaned and sneezed. I didn't know what to do! And then I remembered your unfortunate business card. Unfortunately, I'd thrown it into the garbage earlier, so I had to go back home and look for it in the trash. That was pretty humiliating. But what else could I do? Speaking of which, do you always wear a hat around the house?"

"No!" Farah said. "Definitely not! I'm sick with a . . ."

"Cool apartment. Stupid location. But at least it's a good size. I envy you. I don't have a home anymore. To our homelessness, Bastard!" Go said, raising a toast toward the cat, which was sniffing at a pillow.

"For now, you can sleep here," says Farah, turning red.

"Really? That's not so bad. And anyway, I do know some people nearby."

"The bed's pretty big." Fah went out to the kitchen. "I was thinking I'd fix us something to munch on?"

"Maybe so. Otherwise, soon I'll be worse off than you were that last time. How did that happen? I'm never that far gone after just two bottles of whiskey."

"I can't hear you!" Farah yells. "Maybe some pasta?"

As if she had five other dishes up her sleeve! The only recipe she did have called for the three ingredients she still had from her *A Life Filled with Miracles* period. ("Open your heart and your home! A box of good pasta and a jar of organic sun-dried tomatoes take up significantly less room in your cupboard than they will occupy in the hearts of your friends.")

"Tard? Not there, Little Bastard!" Go is saying in the meantime, trying on the off-navy Hunter rain boots. "Aw hell, I think he might have peed on your pillow."

"No big deal!" Farah smiled. "I just adore the smell of cat pee."

No, no, that's not what she said at all. She didn't hear, she was busy cooking and thinking about herself. She felt as though she were playing herself in a movie. Her hands were shaking. The whole time she was racked with shivers of distrust. It was like in her dreams! Only a little worse, obviously.

"It's ready," she finally said, bringing in the plates. Go sauntered right along the bookshelf, dragging her finger across all the books and CDs.

"Have you ever had bootcakes?" she prattled, digging into her meal. "I have a monstrous hankering for some bootcakes. It's this traditional Yugoslav dish, I don't know how to explain it. A cross between dumplings and flakes, or else . . . Hard to say, you'd have to try it. Anyway, it's the best thing you've ever—"

Here Go choked all of a sudden, leaning over her bowl, and her body seized up in a gag reflex. Her eyes goggled, and her mouth twisted.

After which she spat out a long and quite thick ribbon of hair mixed with pasta.

CHAPTER 23

She turned on the light.

"You disgusting fur ball!" she screamed, throwing a rain boot at the Little Bastard having a stretch. "Get your stinking ass away from my pillow!"

The cat fled to the window. On the table stood the untouched meal and the unfinished whiskey, the props of her defeat. She took a few swigs from the bottle. She collapsed on the bed, in her hat and shoes, and burst into a fierce sob. Could life treat her any more unfairly? Could her humiliation get any deeper?

Forget about the hair, that was the least of it! Ultimately, with a concerted effort, that could still somehow be turned into a joke (a *high-fiber* diet—ha ha ha). But all of a sudden Go had pushed the still-steaming plate aside and said it was tasty, but she needed to take a bath. A bath! She locked herself in the bathroom with the bottle and a telephone and sat there for almost an hour beside the loudly flowing water, in a heated fight with someone. "I'm not going anywhere, you toxic sumbitch!" Farah heard, having settled herself close enough to the door. "Don't look for me! Don't ask where I am! I'm with *somebody,* yeah, somebody close who's offered me help and it has nothing to do with you, you fucking ball-licker!"

Next she had come out wearing Farah's robe. She announced that "Chris was begging her to stop messing around and come to Tania's right away."

"I'm never falling for that again!" she screamed.
"No way," F. said.
"I'm not going there!"
"Don't go, under no circumstances!"

She had felt she was giving her good advice, not actually knowing where it was coming from. She got down to fixing the shower curtain, which had apparently not withstood the fervor of the conversation. The air was blue with humid, acrid steam; on the sink lay numerous cigarette butts with traces of lipstick, which looked like murdered Lego figures. Go was walking around the room and knocking into something from time to time, analyzing aloud the causes and sources of the emotional-sexual conflict she was stuck in, as she put it, "up to her ass." The narrative, which paid rather little mind to its audience, was chaotic, it was convoluted and performed somehow for its own sake, and the rattling off of intimate, not always necessary details lent it a distinct pleasurableness, which grew proportionately with Farah's brick-red blush.

"You're not too warm?" Go finally asked, extinguishing her cigarette on a glass.
"No, no," Fah whispered. "I'm sick in my ears."
"Your ears?!"

For unknown reasons, this prosaic truth really depressed Go. Because, gazing upon Farah with neither distrust nor

139

disdain, she suddenly grew faint. She hung inertly over the armchair, monitoring her iPhone, and from one moment to the next her brow grew overcast with thick clouds of sadness and apathy. Finally she grabbed the *Yogalife* and started flipping through it balefully, like someone whose flight is seventy-eight hours delayed.

"God, where do you get such rags?!" she screamed, tossing the magazine into a corner. "Have you ever let a nasty one rip while 'Greeting the sun'? Ever slip on some spilled muesli? Look out. It says here you might be a *yogaloser!*"

After a quarter hour of looking out the window and sighing, she started to pull on her pants like nothing had happened.

"You going somewhere?" Farah asked, now completely stupefied, making her bed with trembling hands.

"To Tania's," Go said, distributing makeup around her face. "*What of it?*"

"Nothing, really," said Farah, and she took several repulsive swigs of whiskey straight from the bottle.

"You want to come, too?" Go said, more making sure than suggesting. "You could. I'm going to have a hard time with these bags."

"Well, if . . ."

"But under one condition: that we leave Little Bastard with you."

"Little Bastard?"

"His cage is awfully heavy."

"But . . ."

"Try lifting it and say if you want to lug it around!"

"I can't take a cat!"

"Why not? It's just for one night," Go hissed, finishing her drink. "Okay, *no means no*. Nothing to discuss. I'll manage somehow. Keep this collar, too. To me it stinks of cemetery. Bastard! Little Bastard! Come on, we're leaving. They don't want us anywhere. We're going. What a day, maybe I'll get drunk!" she added, resolutely refusing to acknowledge her present state.

CHAPTER 24

I love taking the subway. It makes me feel something on the border between religion and sex. Which allegedly don't share a border at all.

Ernest maintains that it's disgusting, what I'm saying. He can't take it when I make myself into a Björk minus any hint of musical talent, "Oh, I myself don't know why I'm so strange!" and "I'm going to make a necklace from drops of my own juices, and I want you all to call me 'magical woman-tree'!"

But perhaps that's normal when you spend the majority of your time sitting alone in an apartment. I try to work, but instead I eat, or I think up reasons why I cannot write. I struggle, encased in my own head like in a can. The world? What world? From this apartment, the city looks like a model. There's no sound, all it emits is a monotonous wheezing, like the thickest, infinitely agitated string of a contrabass. Then, when I suddenly have somewhere I have to be, something I have to take care of, shock: at every step—people! Six billion other people have been traipsing under my window the whole time, just past my wall. Just past my skull!

When it comes to the subway, the issue is hygienic, epidemiological. I cannot get it into my head that in this postmodern and, in fact, post-physical, *post-real* world, all

of a sudden there's this. Facebook friendships, game con-
sole sports, camera-phone sex, Skype childrearing, dead fish
in the rivers, dead birds in the trees, dead trees, holograms,
space vacations, antibacterial gel and probiotic gel and two-
in-one anti-probiotic gel, and, all of a sudden, amid all that,
the subway car pulls in. Filled to the brim with a roaring,
thumping-pulsing, tangled, importunate, disorganized, mad-
deningly physical human mass!

The doors close, and I'm sealed up in the unmonitored
physiological block. In broad daylight, in a highly developed
country, I adhere the entire surface of my body to those of
other people. I hear the beating of their hearts, the swoosh
of their brains, the murmur of their bloodstreams, I feel the
moistness of their eyes and the turgor pressure of abdomi-
nal cavities absorbed in digestive processes—the monotonous white noise of life, of which I am a part. Everywhere
are ears, polluted pores, liver spots, turbans, perfumes, teeth,
breaths, bacterial flora, open wounds, children's hair, Band-
Aids on calluses, moustaches, which I'm coming to terms
with, banding together with, swirling with, sticking together.
So high does the car's people-saturation seem, it's as though
the membranes separating specific individuals could simply
burst, allowing us to clump together into one great big endless mass.

The doors open at Royal Barber Street, and those who
work there, in the great big Sony office building, are trying
to get out. They writhe, try to detach, get unstuck—to no
avail! I am aghast, mortified by their hysterical shrieks, their
panic-stricken faces, perhaps I even find it amusing. Until.
All of a sudden I come around to the fact that my head is

starting to teem with strange thoughts that I've never had before, suddenly I feel an itch (though "I" is already over-stating it) on the nose of the little Korean woman on my left, and my—or, rather, our—stomach is overflowing with the huge portion of kimchi she'd eaten a short time ago. Meanwhile, some old man is sticking a needle of insulin into my thigh with the hand of the young girl with the yoga mat; someone is grasping disgustedly after the memory of his first time, and somebody else is clawing at our shared armpit. My identity, my beloved collection of bullshit, piled up so eagerly from my memories, thoughts, garbage, tastes, obsessions, and regrets, is absorbed, sucked in, scattered. It disperses, diffuses, dissolves in the ocean of others . . .

Ernest looks at me confusedly when I say this.

But I'll take it, "The Crushing Sensation on Public Transport and the Metaphysical Dread of Being Incorporated into the Great Lump of Humanity"—that's my talk, which I'm going to deliver all around the States if this whole book thing doesn't work out. I'm going to spark endless discussions and congratulations and eat breakfasts in hotels I admire, and in the end I'll receive the Jerzy Kosinski Prize for the Best Lecture Never Delivered in the States.

I've drawn the curtain aside and looked down at the street. The girl with the shaved scalp I'd met in the entry-way—there, she's caught a cab. Farah in her cap—with that jug in her hand—what the hell had they been up to with that Clorox? Some kind of performance art?—on the edge of the sidewalk, swaying on the curb, as over an abyss.

CHAPTER 25

"Wait for me here," Go said, foisting her belongings on Farah. Whereupon she vanished somewhere.

Farah fixed her eyes first on the saltshaker. Then, one by one, she pulled all the napkins out of their holder, tore them into neat squares, and wound each of them into a spindle shape, arranging them alternately with the crumbs into the shape of a little sun around the greasy stain on the tablecloth.

"Tracy, is that you?" someone shouted. It was that guy with the beard from the Lizard's Stomach. "I hardly recognized you!"

He smiled broadly. In this context he seemed so good-natured to her, familiar, almost close.

"It belongs to Go," she shouted across the general hubbub when his gaze hung for a good while on the container of bleach she was holding.

"Can I get you something to drink?" he asked. And he departed, having forgotten to wait for a response.

Tania's is this Yugoslav bar in St. Patrick's. It's the in thing to get all bothered over the antlers they have over there, the paneling, the whiskey wafting of jet fuel, and the silly chandeliers wheezing with dirt-cheap lightbulbs. *It's so atmospheric!* The sickly yellow light lures one into blackmail and assassination, the corners are oozing with the enormity of the kind of wickedness that played out here back when the felt on the pool table was still lustrous and green. Now that the flow of days and economic fluctuations has covered it in a stiff fresco of vomitus and alcohol, it stands slightly off to the side, surrounded by men with drink-swollen faces. In their years of intense struggle with sobriety, they have all lost their facial features, keeping only the most basic paraphernalia, to wit: nose, ears, tobacco-yellow mustache; hours on end they conduct alcoholic negotiations amongst themselves, even when their main thrust has long since vanished in streams of fantastical Yugoslav disco. The sexually disoriented dudes who drop in here, their thighs thinner than my upper arms, take these men as a kind of organic installation art or set piece, a glassless aquarium with great big old fish availing themselves of articulate speech (and not always that).

The eponymous Tania stands behind the bar, an expansive woman in a cardigan with a pearly sheen, with the beautiful, sumptuously made-up face of a saint. She exudes regal dignity, like a Yugoslav tsarina in an internment camp. Her bosom, extending a meter in front of her, could accommodate the heads of fifteen men seeking tenderness and understanding, and the milk from her breasts would taste of garlic and the burgundy she sips from under the counter. Tania's husband died two years ago, and his body has never been found. She allegedly holds on to this dive only in the hope that he'll come back. He'll walk in one day and place his hand on her rear, and she'll turn around and whisper, "Oleg . . . ," nestle her face in his leather jacket, slippery with seaweed and benzene, into his matted hair, full of wriggling eels.

•

146

After an hour had passed, Farah decided to look for Go.

It turned out she was playing foosball in the other half of the joint. "Golly, it's you!" she screamed upon seeing F.; her eyes were already coated in a thick film of drunkenness. She was accompanied by two unusually slack young bucks with half-shut eyes, plus a couple of other people. They all had tight-fitting jeans, tattoos bursting from under their sleeves, and haircuts that in a certain way recalled Farah's from that morning, when she had decided to wear a hat. "This is Farah," Go said, wanting to introduce her, or else simply to remind herself of her name, any way you cut it, the match was just then getting heated, or there'd been a goal, someone had seized Go and begun tossing her around, there was suddenly more of everyone, significantly more, they started to scream, to crowd and crush, and they were even more stylish and fashionable, totally as though they'd peeled off from the pages of subversive fashion magazines and, with the parachutes of their low-cut shirts, touched down on planet Earth, right into Tania's. Oh, please, they had no time to hang out with this Farah girl, ordinary, unstylish, consisting entirely of flaws, resembling a vegetable or animal, or a child among many, or scrambled eggs, she wandered the suburbs of their style and sanctity with a container of bleach and a fake, impossibly strained smile holding on by its last thread . . .

The match continued, oblivious to the world, and in it she was playing for Team Air. No one was looking at her now, her smile snapped like undersized panties, exposing her face, disoriented, warped by distrust and pain. Nothing for her here, she should turn on her heels and just get going, take the subway, go back home, to her own life. After all, she had time off; she could go . . . to sleep, at the least. Or to the mall, it was mid-October, after all, the Christmas sales were sure to have begun already. But Farah didn't have the strength to go anywhere. Where would she go? What for? She was a failure, an exile from the land of dreams. She took a glass of the best wine (Carlo Rossi) and wet her whistle, wincing.

And just then, unexpectedly, the whole shitstorm broke.

First, from the general din, from the palimpsest of drunken gripes and brags, there emerged several raised voices. One of them belonged with utter certainty to Go. There was some kind of commotion by the foosball table. They were arguing loudly about something and reassuring each other, but the chemical substances in the opponents' bloodstreams were evidently complicating both the one thing and the other.

Farah moved in closer. Go was arguing with one of those dudes, who was being held back by another, and who was who there was no way to confirm, all three were mad as dogs, ready to leap on each other, cling to each other's throats, and at the same time they were calling each other back to reason, which brought about an escalation of the conflict.

Which concerned some uncle from Yugoslavia. According to Go, her Uncle Hank was among those playing pool; before he'd gone to the dogs, he'd reportedly been a policeman and made a mean peas and carrots. Chris's boyfriend, whichever one of them he was, had poked fun at that or had in some other manner cast doubt on it, but one thing's for sure: everyone had long since forgotten the potential Uncle Hank. He'd gone back to Bohemia, to Belarus, or some other state in the Former Yugoslavia, taking M&Ms for his grandchildren and two pairs of acid-washed jeans for his youngest son, whereas the conflict, like a blaze, had long since spread to matters more general.

"She's fucked-up, I swear," Chris's boyfriend squealed. He had fingernail tracks on his cheek. "Ask her for the weather or directions, and she'll tell you: pierogi, borscht, and cabbage soup. Who can stand it? And that affected accent of hers. Who's finally going to tell this idiot she's not from some fucking Poland?!"

"I used to have a neighbor who was from Poland, get it?" Go screamed. "So I happen to know a little about the accent. Besides, I think it's cute being from Poland! And it doesn't have shit to do with you."

"If there's one thing you have, Margo, it's a daddy with influence," the boyfriend screamed. "Not to mention the shit between your ears."

Now that must have struck a nerve with her. She rolled her eyes dully and drenched the boyfriend with a glass of whiskey. Clawing spasmodically at the air, she started wailing that it shouldn't matter to him, since he's jealous that he hadn't come up with all of it himself. He envies her because he wasn't the one who started the trend of being from the Former Yugoslavia, and he's constantly trying to bully and undermine her; it's her identity, it has shit to do with him; only she can determine who she is and who she isn't, and *Loraz is the best fucking grocery chain in the neighborhood,* a company that looks after its employees and doesn't artificially inflate its prices, and if he doesn't believe her, just go compare at D'Agostini. To wrap up, she stated that she was now going to the river to drown herself, and no one was going to stop her now, since she'd given them plenty of warning already—*plenty* of warning! And just one more thing: if the press wants to know who bears the guilt for her death, then the guilt belongs to—and here she screamed out two names that Farah didn't entirely understand . . .

. . . because that was just when she reached Go with her things and the aforementioned container and . . .

But Go shoved her into the foosball table.

"Leave me alone, you fucking psycho!"

At which point Fah removed her hat, revealing her mauled skull.

"Now what do you say?" she said, upon which she performed the popular motion of turning a crank around her temple.

And then, her Louboutins pounding, she ran out into an evening redolent of river and scrap metal.

CHAPTER 26

Psycho!

Farah was sobbing, nothing could calm her down, she didn't want to calm down, she had no reason to. She hated herself, hated herself with all her might! How could Go humiliate her like that, how could she turn against her, though she herself had been saying a moment earlier that she had no one else! How could she take her naked heart and flush it down the toilet, when it was still warm, still beating! She could have killed her sooner, yes, killed her, if she'd intended to play her like that. Oh, how it hurt, she couldn't breathe, she was suffocating, she wanted to not exist! The cat, either out of sympathy or else simply out of hunger, issued a monotonous, plaintive mew, such that you could come away with the impression that it was mocking her frustration, making fun of her, narrowing its bored eyes.

Just then Farah discovered on her pillow a sizeable wet stain that smelled in no way of tears.

"You pig," she grumbled through her teeth. "You disgusting wormy little shit."

CHAPTER 27

"Twenty-four-year-old Margo Lee, daughter of influential grocery-store magnate and increasingly active political figure Matthew Loraz, was detained last night by police. She had been at the wheel of a truck speeding down the city streets, despite being totally drunk and without a driver's license. The vehicle had been stolen.

Margo Lee is the youngest daughter of Matthew Loraz, a likely candidate in next year's mayoral election. His older daughter, Mary Ann Charlotte, is a high-powered attorney, and his son Robert directs a popular travel agency. Will the youngest Miss Loraz's excesses hold up her dad's career just as it is picking up steam?"

"Who would have thought; Loraz is a good chain!" Joanne said, pulling down the cups of her swimsuit to check her tan. "In fact, that's where I always buy my groceries."

The news had ended.

"In my opinion, they're the best food stores around. D'Agostini doesn't come close; they may have a wider selection, but they're significantly more expensive! Daim Bars, those little things are like four bucks, don't you think that's a bit much?" she asked, turning off the radio, because, too bad, they'd just started up with "Tip-Tap Faucets," the scourge of mankind.

"Speaking of which: I had a dream about Farah," the Hungarianist said.

"I didn't dream about anything."

"Something had dragged me under the water, and that's when I saw her: she was like a mermaid or something . . ."

"Gross."

"I have to look up what that means in a dream book."

"You want me to tell you what it means?"

"What?"

"That your subconscious wanted to stare at her tits. Who's going to be first in the water?"

CHAPTER 28

Farah was lying motionless and empty at the bottom amid the garbage and old newspapers, looking at her cat-scratched hands. All of a sudden, some sprightly, cold little hand grabbed her by the wrist. It was that mermaid, the one that, once upon a time, had shown her the drain. She'd pulled the pajama bottoms she'd gypped Farah out of onto her head like a veil, the legs hung down in ear shapes along the sides of her bluish face, and her eyes were suitably cheerful and mendacious:

"Hey there, chin up!" she said in her jauntily hoarse voice. "Everybody knows those refugees from the Former Yugoslavia are frightfully bonkers over hats!"

Farah gave her a contemptuous look and sat down, shaking off shreds of some old wallpaper.

"I remember this one guy, he got shit-faced and lay down in a rowboat and got covered in water. I swim up, and he says: 'Hey there, cutie, have a drink with me, I still have a bit of booze here, yada yada.' We drink, we drink some more, and I says to him: 'Poland is the most beautiful country I've ever seen'; though actually I've never been there, but I was already seriously smashed, and I wanted to make him feel good. 'Fields full of poppies, the people are rapacious, but warm—they kiss bread when it falls.'

"'What do you know!' the Yugoslav roared. 'It's the stinkiest vale of tears on the face of the earth.'

"To which I, because I wanted to be nice and agreeable, said: 'Well, it does indeed have an inhuman stink.' To which he said: 'Think it stinks, do you? You little fucker!'

"It was a lucky thing he was dead, because he wanted to strangle me with a pickle!"

Farah had no response. Her heart was so empty that it gave her the impression that she was dead.

"We found a diver on the reef," the mermaid said like it was no big deal, "and the girls feel like dancing. We have a tambourine and genuine samba dresses. Maybe you'll stop by?"

She swam off in her awkward manner, swinging her tail to only one side and flapping the pajama legs. Farah, for whatever reason, swam after her. Maybe she'd been lured by the water's phosphorescent turquoise, beguiled by the wavering, gossamer threads of sunlight and the plastic bags billowing majestically like jellyfish; and maybe she swam just to swim, to use up her strength, her feeling, her breath . . .

They descended deeper, where it was now dark. Other mermaids immediately appeared, their teeth sparse and faces mottled: they were trying to sit the diver upright, but time and again he sagged under the weight of the oxygen tank, and they joyously welcomed the opportunity for fresh entertainment.

A moment later Farah was ringed in a tight circle, to welcome her, to play with her, they were coquettish, ready for a good time. They tickled her, tittering metallically. Anyway, maybe they had only the best intentions.

"Rub-a-dub!" they screamed, pretending that they were scrubbing her like a baby with a piece of an old hand broom and laughing till they cried. "Splish-splash!" Despite this, the game was less and less fun.

As happens, the growing tension, the unease, and finally the terror and entirely open resistance of the victims in such instances always intensify the perversity and ill will, and not infrequently they succeed in transforming an innocent game into a grim, drawn-out execution, the cruelty of which later astounds even the executioner. Before she knew it, her body was being felt up by dozens of cold hands, busy as worms; everything was spinning faster and faster, she saw their faces all around, bluish, waterlogged, almost flat, free of projections, cleansed of features, seaweed-smeared, dirty, gross, horrible . . .

"Make them leave me alone!" Farah was screaming.

"Oh stop, they're just pleased you came," the other one screamed back from a distance, from quite a distance. "I'm leaving you with them. I have to help my sister: she's just laid her eggs."

Meanwhile, amid monkey-like shrieks, the mermaids were fighting each other over the things they'd snatched from her. One of them was already off somewhere at full tilt in her hat, others were tearing each other's hair out over one of her shoes, and for this reason they were nearly bald. In the meantime, one had dug a roll of duct tape out from somewhere; amid the shrieks and wails, their icy hands had grasped Farah by the legs, binding them together and wrapping them top to bottom in plastic wrap. In their customary manner, they stuck the plate of an electric stove on her feet, so that it sort of passed as a tail. They left her only the drab H&M bra, and to mock her they placed a crown on her head made from a brass ventilation grill. She tried to call for help: she saw the old invalid mermaid who was observing this torture with stoic calm, probably not seeing anything and poking around her teeth with a broken checker; she had the braid of F's hair, thick and shiny, secured to the top of her gray head with an infantile pin . . .

She wanted to scream, but she only choked and went limp in their arms, ever weaker and more passive.

Ratatatatat!

Shots rang out suddenly, unexpectedly, from who knows where.

CHAPTER 29

Albert was banging his fist on the door. He had called ear-lier, but she wasn't opening. He knew she was there; she always was. He heard her tiptoeing up to the door.

"Open up!" he said.

"What are you doing here?!" she screamed.

"I have to tell you something."

"Go away," she said hoarsely.

All he wanted to tell her was what he'd dreamed—he had to. A couple of days ago the doctor had switched him over to Vaxylan—similar, at any rate, to the 20 mg Xavylan—after which, whenever he shut his eyes, his head swarmed with freakishly real images oversaturated with color. And it's not important, but yesterday he woke up in the middle of the night on his Caesar-salad-dressing-stained Ikea sofa bed, cuddling up to an unfinished bottle of cola, but when he tried to feel his way with his foot to the chip-crumb-scat-tered parquet floor, he understood that he was surrounded by a sort of ocean. Vaxylan delays one's reaction time some-what, and it drives a person into this particular nonbrilliance, a matte half-lethargy, so he gawked at all of this, somewhat surprised when he suddenly spotted some kind of scuffle beneath the water.

He saw it underneath him, like it was covered in glass, at a slowed tempo: Farah, hairless, in her underwear, like a puppet being carried somewhere by gap-toothed, rabid, perfectly animated mermaids. They were hideous, revolting, with bluish skin, through which you could see their veins and their weird, nonhumanlike organs. The quality of the graphics, the realism of the images, were so high it started to make him queasy. He didn't know how to swim, and he hesitated a moment, but he ultimately stuffed his PlayStation controller into the waistband of his boxers, grabbed a Domino's Pizza box, and, using it as a kickboard—he'd learned this trick from swim school—he charged in among the scuffling monsters and started shooting.

Ratatatatat!

He was sure he'd managed to take down several right away: he saw their pockmarked, sickly faces splattering into bloody pixels, the pinkish gore bursting from toothless mouths. They fell limp toward the bottom, trailing cyclamen ribbons of blood, while the rest fled amid screams and shrieks, flapping their mangy tails to hide among crews of wicker beach chairs and mangled yachts. Dozens of their stupid, animal-vigilant eyes were following him now, twinkling like a fistful of fake diamonds tossed in the garbage. He stuck the controller back into the waistband of his boxers and thought that this was a high level of carnage even for him; nothing good would come of staying here long; he grabbed Farah by the hand and pulled her up.

She was scratched and unconscious, but once she came around she immediately swam faster than he, making deft use of her tail. Now they were closer to shore, where the water was clearer, cleaner, the environs pastel-colored, almost pretty; they were surrounded by big-eyed silver sardines, dispirited halibut, schools of flickering chocolate wrappers and orange peels. They had to pass some kind of beach resort, they saw the legs of people taking a dip and, for a laugh, even tickled a few of the especially pretty ones on the foot. Suddenly, Farah stopped and observed the people swimming, still sort of hesitating, but there was something she couldn't resist.

"Wait a sec," she said. There was a butt suspended in the water not far from them that was packed tightly in Sponge Bob bottoms, and tacked onto that were over-thin legs with a seam drawn down their whole length; next to them swung the black-tanned, scrawny stems of some guy. Swimming up to them, Farah yanked all of them so violently that the two silhouettes, struggling pathetically, dropped beneath the surface, issuing fountains of hysterical little bubbles. All Albert remembered was the woman's hair, which blew up like a bomb under the water—a strange color, sort of an artificial chestnut.

Oh, he wanted like hell to tell her all this now. Why couldn't she open the door?

At last he heard the rattle of the lock.

"*Get out of here,*" Farah said calmly, coldly. She was holding antibacterial gel; her arms were scratched all the way up past her elbows.

CHAPTER 30

I ran into him in the elevator, he looked like an abused dog. In a T-shirt and boxers, with ketchup at the corner of his mouth, he must have left home in a great hurry; on the side of his head, his hair formed a ball of art nouveau intricacy; he had a PlayStation controller tucked into the waist of his drawers. Dejected, he'd forgotten to press his button, and he was descending with me toward the ground floor.

It was a cloudy morning, and that's why I was surprised at the sight: nearly in the middle of the road there lay a cat with a white ruff, completely motionless. I turned back into the entryway, went home, and, even though Ernest was looking at me with tremendous doubt, I sat down at my computer.

There was a white-ruffed cat lying in the street in front of the apartment building—I wrote then—neither warming itself in the sun, nor really even alive, as we might surmise from the fact that there was no sun, nor any other reason to lie there among speeding cars.

Some patrol car will eventually come and take him away, Farah thought, and, tugging at her pajama bottoms, which had given her a wedgie, she went back to reading.

Dorota Masłowska is a renowned, multi-award-winning Polish writer, playwright, and journalist born in 1983. Hailed as the greatest young writer in Poland as well as Polish literature's *enfant terrible*, Masłowska received the prestigious Polityka Prize for her debut novel, *Snow White and Russian Red*, published when she was just nineteen years old (and published in English by Grove Atlantic). The book garnered massive critical acclaim in Poland, has been translated into over a dozen languages, and was made into a movie directed by Xawery Żuławski. Since then, she has written several novels and plays and has become a celebrated literary figure in Poland. *Honey, I Killed the Cats*, her second novel to be published in English, has been adapted for stage.

Benjamin Paloff is the author of *Lost in the Shadow of the Word (Space, Time and Freedom in Interwar Eastern Europe)* (Northwestern University Press), named the 2018 Best Book in Literary/Cultural Studies by the American Association of Teachers of Russian and East European Languages. He has also published two collections of poems, *And His Orchestra* (2015) and *The Politics* (2011), both from Carnegie Mellon University Press. He has translated several books from Polish and Czech, including works by Richard Weiner, Marek Bienczyk, and Andrzej Sosnowski. He has twice received grants from the National Endowment for the Arts—in poetry as well as translation—and has been a fellow of the US Fulbright Programs, the Stanford Humanities Center, and the Michigan Society of Fellows. He is currently a professor at the University of Michigan.

Thank you all
for your support.
We do this for you,
and could not do
it without you.

DEEP
VELLUM

PARTNERS

pixel ||| texel

ALLRED
CAPITAL MANAGEMENT
of
RAYMOND JAMES®

AVAILABLE NOW FROM DEEP VELLUM

MICHÈLE AUDIN · *One Hundred Twenty-One Days*
translated by Christiana Hills · FRANCE

BAE SUAH · *Recitation*
translated by Deborah Smith · SOUTH KOREA

EDUARDO BERTI · *The Imagined Land*
translated by Charlotte Coombe · ARGENTINA

CARMEN BOULLOSA · *Texas: The Great Theft* · *Before* · *Heavens on Earth*
translated by Samantha Schnee · Peter Bush · Shelby Vincent · MEXICO

Cleave, Sarah, ed. · *Banthology: Stories from Banned Nations* · IRAN, IRAQ,
LIBYA, SOMALIA, SUDAN, SYRIA & YEMEN

LEILA S. CHUDORI · *Home*
translated by John H. McGlynn · INDONESIA

DOROTA MASŁOWSKA · *Honey, I Killed the Cats*
translated by Benjamin Paloff · POLAND

ANANDA DEVI · *Eve Out of Her Ruins*
translated by Jeffrey Zuckerman · MAURITIUS

ALISA GANIEVA · *Bride and Groom* · *The Mountain and the Wall*
translated by Carol Apollonio · RUSSIA

ANNE GARRÉTA · *Sphinx* · *Not One Day*
translated by Emma Ramadan · FRANCE

JÓN GNARR · *The Indian* · *The Pirate* · *The Outlaw*
translated by Lytton Smith · ICELAND

KIM YIDEUM · *Blood Sisters*
translated by Ji yoon Lee · SOUTH KOREA

GOETHE · *The Golden Goblet: Selected Poems*
translated by Zsuzsanna Ozsváth and Frederick Turner · GERMANY

NOEMI JAFFE · *What are the Blind Men Dreaming?*
translated by Julia Sanches & Ellen Elias-Bursac · BRAZIL

CLAUDIA SALAZAR JIMÉNEZ · *Blood of the Dawn*
translated by Elizabeth Bryer · PERU

JUNG YOUNG MOON · *Vaseline Buddha*
translated by Yewon Jung · SOUTH KOREA

JOSEFINE KLOUGART · *Of Darkness*
translated by Martin Aitken · DENMARK

YANICK LAHENS · *Moonbath*
translated by Emily Gogolak · HAITI

FORTHCOMING FROM DEEP VELLUM

ANNE GARRÉTA · *In/concrete*
translated by Emma Ramadan · FRANCE

C.F. RAMUZ · *Jean-Luc Persecuted*
translated by Olivia Baes · SWITZERLAND

DMITRY LIPSKEROV · *The Tool and the Butterflies*
translated by Reilly Costigan-Humes & Isaac Stackhouse Wheeler · RUSSIA

FOWZIA KARIMI · *Above Us the Milky Way: An Illuminated Alphabet* · USA

GORAN PETROVIĆ · *At the Lucky Hand, aka The Sixty-Nine Drawers*
translated by Peter Agnone · SERBIA

JESSICA SCHIEFAUER · *Girls Lost*
translated by Saskia Vogel · SWEDEN

JUNG YOUNG MOON · *Seven Samurai Swept Away in a River*
translated by Yewon Jung · SOUTH KOREA

LEYLA ERBIL · *A Strange Woman*
translated by Nermin Menemencioğlu · TURKEY

MAGDA CARNECI · *FEM*
translated by Sean Cotter · ROMANIA

MARIO BELLATIN · *Mrs. Murakami's Garden*
translated by Heather Cleary · MEXICO

MATHILDE CLARK · *Lone Star*
translated by Martin Aitken · DENMARK

MÄRTA TIKKANEN · *The Love Story of the Century*
translated by Stina Katchadourian · FINLAND

MIKE SOTO · *A Grave Is Given Supper: Poems* · USA

MIRCEA CĂRTĂRESCU · *Solenoid*
translated by Sean Cotter · ROMANIA

PERGENTINO JOSÉ · *Red Ants: Stories*
translated by Tom Bunstead and the author · MEXICO

TAISIA KITAISKAIA · *The Nightgown & Other Poems* · USA

TATIANA RYCKMAN · *The Ancestry of Objects* · USA